# Have you got all of Enid Blyton's FAMOUS FIVE books?

(*Also available as dramatised recordings on CD)

H46 587 727 6

# A Note from Enid Blyton's Granddaughter

Welcome to the new edition of The Famous Five series by Enid Blyton. There are 21 books in the collection, a whole world of mystery and adventure to explore. My grandmother, Enid Blyton, wrote her first Famous Five Book, 'Five on a Treasure Island' in 1942. That was in the middle of World War Two (1939–1945). In the story, Julian, Dick and Anne meet their cousin Georgina and her dog, Timmy, for the first time. They soon learn *never* to call her Georgina. Together they explore tunnels and caves, discover hidden passageways and solve crimes.

I first met the Famous Five in a recording of 'Five have a Mystery to Solve'. Julian, Dick, George, Anne and Timmy have developed a love of sausages and can't seem to get enough of them. The sausages are put on hold when a lady knocks at the door of Kirrin Cottage. She has come to ask if the Five could keep her young grandson company in a remote cottage while she is away. The adventure begins as soon as they see the mysterious 'Whispering Island' as they cycle to the cottage to meet the grandson, Wilfred.

Timmy has always been my favourite character. He is the best judge of personality and when he is around, everything seems much safer; not that I am scared of adventure! Since watching the Famous Five television series in the 1970s, which cast Timmy as a Border-Collie sheep dog, I have always wanted to have a Border-Collie.

Who do you think you'll like best?

*Sophie Smallwood, 14 June 2010*

# *Five Have
Plenty Of Fun*

# Enid Blyton

# THE FAMOUS FIVE

## Five Have Plenty Of Fun

Hodder
Children's
Books

A division of Hachette Children's Books

Enid Blyton ® Famous Five ®
Copyright © 2010 Chorion Rights Ltd
All rights reserved
'Foreword' copyright Sophie Smallwood 2010

First published in Great Britain in 1954 by Hodder and Stoughton

This revised edition first published in 2010 by Hodder Children's Books

With thanks to Rachel Elliot

The right of Enid Blyton to be identified as the Author of
the Work has been asserted by her in accordance with the
Copyright, Designs and Patents Act 1988.

2

A Catalogue record for this book is available from the British Library

ISBN 978 0 340 93172 1

Typeset by Avon DataSet Ltd, Bidford-on-Avon, Warwickshire

Printed and bound in Great Britain by Clays Ltd, St Ives plc

The paper and board used in this paperback by Hodder Children's Books
are natural recyclable products made from wood grown in sustainable
forests. The manufacturing processes conform to the environmental
regulations of the country of origin.

Hodder Children's Books
a division of Hachette Children's Books
338 Euston Road, London NW1 3BH
An Hachette UK company
www.hachette.co.uk

# Contents

# 1  At Kirrin Cottage

'I feel as if we've been at Kirrin for about a month already!' said Anne, stretching herself out on the warm sand, and digging her toes in. 'And we've only just come!'

'Yes – it's funny how we settle down at Kirrin so quickly,' said Dick. 'We only came yesterday, and I agree with you, Anne – it seems as if we've been here ages. I love Kirrin.'

'I hope this weather lasts out the three weeks we've got left of the holiday,' said Julian, rolling away from Timmy, who was pawing at him, trying to make him play. 'Go away, Timmy. You're too energetic. We've swum, had a run, played ball – and that's enough for a little while. Go and play with the crabs!'

'Woof!' said Timmy, disgusted. Then he pricked up his ears as he heard a tinkling noise from the promenade. He barked again.

'Trust Timmy to hear the ice-cream man,' said

Dick. 'Anyone want an ice-cream?'

Everyone did, so Anne collected the money and went off to get the ice-creams, Timmy close at her heels. She came back with five tubs of ice-cream, Timmy jumping up at her all the way.

'I can't think of anything nicer than lying down on hot sand with the sun on every part of my body, eating an ice-cream, and knowing there are still three weeks' holiday in front of us – at Kirrin too!' said Dick.

'Yes. It's wonderful,' said Anne. 'It's a pity your dad has visitors today, George. Who are they? Have we got to dress up for them?'

'I don't think so,' said George. 'Timmy, you've eaten your ice-cream in one gulp. What a waste!'

'When are these people coming?' asked Dick.

'About half past twelve,' said George. 'They're coming to lunch – but thankfully Dad told Mum he didn't want a pack of children gobbling all around him and his friends at lunch, so Mum said we could go in at half past twelve, say hello and then go off again with a picnic basket.'

'I think your dad has some good ideas at times,' said Dick. 'I suppose they're some scientist friends of his?'

'Yes. Dad's working on some great scheme with these two men,' said George. 'One of them's a genius, apparently, and has thought of an amazing new idea.'

'What kind of new idea?' said Julian, lazily, holding out his fingertips for Timmy to lick off smears of ice-cream. 'A cheap rocket to take us on day trips to the moon – or a new bomb – or . . .'

'No, I *think* it's something that'll give us heat, light and power for almost nothing!' said George. 'I heard Dad say that it's the simplest and best idea anyone had ever worked out, and he's really excited about it. He called it a "gift to mankind" and said he was proud to have anything to do with it.'

'Uncle Quentin's very clever, isn't he?' said Anne.

George's father was the uncle of Julian, Dick and Anne, and they were cousins to George – short for Georgina. Once more they had all come down to Kirrin for part of their holiday, the last three weeks.

George's father was certainly clever. All the same, George sometimes wished that he was a more *ordinary* parent, one who'd play games, and not be so horrified at shouting and laughter and silly jokes. He always made a fuss when George's mother insisted that George should have her cousins to stay.

'Noisy, rowdy, yelling kids!' he said. 'I'll lock myself in my study and stay there!'

'All right,' said his wife. 'You do that. But you know perfectly well that they'll be out practically all day long. George *must* have other children to stay sometimes, and her three cousins are the nicest ones I know. George loves having them here.'

The four cousins were very careful not to upset George's father. He had a very hot temper and shouted at the top of his voice when he was angry. Still, as Julian said, he really couldn't *help* being a genius, and geniuses weren't ordinary people.

'Especially *scientific* geniuses who might easily blow up the whole world in a fit of temper,' said Julian, solemnly.

'Well, I wish he wouldn't keep blowing *me* up if I let a door bang, or set Timmy barking,' said George.

'That's only to keep his hand in,' said Dick.

'Just a bit of practice at blowing up!'

'Don't be an idiot,' said George. 'Does anyone feel like another swim?'

'No. But I don't mind going and lying in the very edge of the sea, and letting the waves there just curl over me,' said Dick. 'I'm absolutely baked lying here.'

'It *sounds* lovely,' said Anne. 'But the hotter you are the colder the water feels.'

'Come on!' said Dick, getting up. 'I'll hang my tongue out and pant like Timmy soon.'

They all went down to the edge of the water and lay down flat in the tiny curling waves there. Anne gave a little shriek.

'It feels icy! I knew it would. I can't lie down in it yet – I can only sit up!'

However they were soon all lying full-length in the shallow waves at the edge of the sea, sliding down the sand a little every now and again as the tide ebbed farther from them. It was lovely to feel the cool fingers of the sea on every part of them.

Suddenly Timmy barked. He wasn't in the water with them, but was just at the edge. He thought that lying down in the sea was completely unnecessary! George raised her head.

'What's the matter?' she said. 'There's nobody coming.'

But Dick had heard something too. He sat up hurriedly. 'I think that's someone ringing a bell for us. It sounds like the bell from Kirrin Cottage!'

'But it *can't* be lunch-time yet!' said Anne.

'It must be,' said Julian, leaping up. 'Oh no! This is what comes of leaving my watch in my pocket! I should have remembered that time at Kirrin goes more quickly than anywhere else!'

He ran up the beach to his things and took his watch from his pocket.

'It's one o'clock!' he yelled. 'In fact, it's a minute past. Hurry up, we'll be really late!'

'Oh no!' said George. 'Mum won't be at all pleased with us, because those two scientist people will be there!'

They collected their things and raced up the beach. It wasn't very far to Kirrin Cottage, fortunately, and they were soon running in at the front gate. There was a very large car outside, one of the latest American models. But there was no time to examine it!

They trailed in quietly at the garden door.

George's mother met them, looking rather cross.

'Sorry, Aunt Fanny,' said Julian. 'Please forgive us. It was my fault. I'm the only one with a watch.'

'Are we *really* late?' asked Anne. 'Have you begun lunch yet? Would you like us just to take our picnic basket and slip off without interrupting?'

'No,' said her aunt. 'Fortunately your uncle's still in his study with his friends. I've sounded the gong once but I don't expect they've even *heard* it! I rang the bell for you because I thought that any moment they might come out, and your uncle would be cross if you weren't there just to say hello!'

'But Dad's friends don't *usually* want to see us,' said George, surprised.

'Well, one of them has a girl a bit younger than you, George – younger than Anne too, I think,' said her mother. 'And he asked to see you all, because his daughter's going to your school next term.'

'We'd better hurry up and have a bit of a wash then,' said Julian – but at that very moment the study door opened, and his Uncle Quentin came out with two men.

'Hello – are these your kids?' said one of the men, stopping.

'They've just come in from the beach,' said Aunt Fanny hurriedly. 'I'm afraid they're not really fit to be seen. I—'

'Great snakes!' said the man. 'Don't you dare to apologise for kids like these! I never saw such an amazing lot in my life – they're wunnerful!'

He spoke with an American accent, and beamed all over his face. The children warmed to him at once. He turned to George's father.

'These all yours?' he asked. 'I bet you're proud of them!'

'They're not all mine,' said Uncle Quentin, looking completely horrified at the thought. 'Only this one is mine,' and he put his hand on George's shoulder. 'The others are nephews and a niece.'

'Well, you've got a fine boy,' said the American, ruffling George's short curls.

As a rule she hated people who did that, but because he mistook her for a boy, she grinned happily!

'My girl Berta's going to your school,' he said to Anne. 'Give her a bit of help, will you? She'll be scared stiff at first.'

'Of course I will,' said Anne, taking a liking to the huge loud-voiced American. He didn't look a bit like a scientist. The other man did, though. He was round-shouldered and wore owl-like glasses, and, as Uncle Quentin often did, he stared into the distance as if he wasn't hearing a single word that anyone said.

Uncle Quentin thought this gossiping had lasted long enough. He waved the children away.

'Come and have lunch,' he said to the other men.

The second man followed him at once, but the big American stayed behind. He thrust his hand into his pocket and brought out a coin. He gave it to Anne.

'Spend that on yourselves,' he said. 'And be kind to my Berta, won't you?'

He disappeared into the dining room and shut the door with a loud bang.

'What will Dad say to a bang like *that*!' said George, with a sudden giggle. 'I like him, don't you? That must be *his* car outside. I can't imagine the other man even riding a bike, let alone driving a car!'

'Children – take your picnic basket and *go*!'

said Aunt Fanny, urgently. 'I *must* run and see that everything is all right!'

She thrust a big basket into Julian's hands, and disappeared into the dining room. Julian grinned as he felt the weight of the basket.

'Come on,' he said. 'This feels good! Back to the beach, everyone!'

## 2  A visitor in the night

The Five were on the beach in two minutes, and Julian undid the basket. It was full of neatly packed sandwiches, and packets of biscuits and chocolate. A bag contained ripe plums, and there were two bottles of lemonade.

'Home-made!' said Dick, taking it out. 'And icy cold. And what's this? A fruitcake – a *whole* fruitcake – we're in luck.'

'Woof,' said Timmy, approvingly, and sniffed inside the basket.

Wrapped in brown paper were some biscuits and a bone, together with a small pot of paste. George undid the packet.

'*I* packed these for you, Timmy,' she said. 'Say thank you!'

Timmy licked her so lavishly that she cried out for mercy.

'Pass me the towel, Ju!' she said. 'Timmy's made my face all wet. Get away now, Timmy –

you've thanked me enough! Get *away*, I said. How can I spread paste on your biscuits if you stick your nose into the pot all the time?'

'You spoil Timmy,' said Anne. 'All right, all right – you needn't scowl at me, George! I agree that he's *worth* spoiling. Take your bone a *bit* farther away from me, Tim – it's smelly!'

They were soon eating sardine sandwiches with tomatoes, and egg-and-lettuce sandwiches after that. Then they started on the fruitcake and the lemonade.

'I don't know why people ever have table meals when they can have picnics,' said Dick. 'Think of Uncle and Aunt and those two men tucking into a hot meal indoors on a day like this!'

'I liked that big American,' said George.

'Aha! We all know why,' said Dick, annoyingly. 'He thought you were a boy. Will you ever grow out of that, George?'

'Timmy's trying to get at the cake!' said Anne. 'Quick, George, stop him!'

They all lay back on the sand after their picnic, and Julian began a long story of a trick that he and Dick had played on their form teacher at school. He was very annoyed because nobody laughed at the funny part, and sat up to see why.

'All asleep!' he said, in disgust. Then he tilted his head just as Timmy pricked up his ears. A loud roaring noise came to him.

'Just the American revving up his car, do you think, Tim?' said Julian. The boy stood up and saw the great car roaring down the sea road.

The day was too hot to do anything but laze. The Five were quite content to do that on their first day together again. Soon they'd want to plan all kinds of things, but the first day at Kirrin was a day for picking up old threads, teasing Timmy, getting into the feel of things again, as Dick said.

Dick and Julian had been abroad for four weeks, and Anne had been away to camp and had had a school friend to stay with her at home afterwards. George had been alone at Kirrin so it was wonderful for the Five to meet together once more for three whole summer weeks. At Kirrin too, Kirrin by the sea, with its lovely beach, its good boating – and its exciting little island across Kirrin Bay!

As usual the first day or two passed in a kind of dream, and then the children began to plan exciting things to do.

'We'll go to Kirrin Island again,' said Dick. 'We haven't been there for ages.'

'We'll go fishing in Lobster Cove,' said Julian.

'We'll go and explore some of the caves in the cliffs,' said George. 'I meant to do that these holidays, but somehow it's no fun going alone.'

On the third day, just as they were finishing making their beds, the phone rang.

'I'll go!' yelled Julian to his aunt, and went to answer it. An urgent voice spoke at the other end.

'Who's that? Oh, you, Julian – you're Quentin's nephew, aren't you? Listen, tell your uncle I'm coming over tonight – yes, tonight. Latish, say. Tell him to wait up for me. It's important.'

'But, don't you want to speak to him yourself?' said Julian, surprised. 'I'll fetch him, if you'll—'

But the line had gone dead. Julian was puzzled. The man hadn't even given his name – but Julian had recognised the voice. It was the big, cheery American who had come to see his uncle two days before! What had happened? What was all the excitement about?

He went to find his uncle but he wasn't in his study. So he found his aunt instead.

'Aunt Fanny,' he said, 'I *think* that was the big American on the phone – the one who came to lunch the other day. He said I was to tell Uncle Quentin that he was coming here tonight – late, he said – and that Uncle was to wait up for him, because it was important.'

'Dear me!' said his aunt, startled. 'Is he going to stay the night then? We've no bedroom free now you and the others are here.'

'He didn't say, Aunt Fanny,' said Julian. 'I'm really sorry not to be able to tell you any details – but just as I was saying I'd fetch Uncle Quentin, he rang off – in the middle of what I was saying.'

'How mysterious!' said his aunt. 'And how annoying. *How* can I put him up, if he wants to stay? I suppose he'll come roaring down at midnight in that enormous car of his. I just hope nothing's gone wrong with this latest work your uncle is doing. I know it's very important.'

'Perhaps Uncle will know the American's phone number and he can ring him up to find out a bit more,' said Julian, helpfully. 'Where's Uncle?'

'He's gone down to the post office, I think,' said his aunt. 'I'll tell him when he gets back.'

Julian told the others about the mysterious

phone call. Dick was pleased.

'I didn't have a chance of getting a good look at that enormous car the other day,' he said. 'I think I'll keep awake tonight till the American comes and then nip down and have a look at it. I bet it's got more gadgets on the dashboard than any car I've ever seen!'

Uncle Quentin appeared to be as surprised as anyone else at the phone call, and was inclined to blame Julian for not finding out more details.

'What's he want now?' he demanded, almost as if Julian ought to know! 'I fixed everything up with him the other day. *Every*thing! Each of us three has his own part to do. Mine's the least important, as it happens – and his is the most important. He took all the papers away with him; he can't have left any behind. Coming down in the middle of the night like this – extraordinary!'

None of the children except Dick meant to stay awake and listen for the American's coming. Dick put on his bedside light and took up a book to read. He knew he'd fall asleep and not wake up for any noise, if he didn't somehow keep himself wide awake!

He listened as he read, his ear alert to hear the car. Eleven o'clock came – then midnight struck. He listened to the twelve dongs from the big grandfather clock in the hall. Uncle Quentin wouldn't be pleased that his visitor was so late!

He yawned, and turned over his page. He read on and on. Half past twelve. One o'clock. Then he thought he heard a sound downstairs and opened his door. Yes – it was Uncle Quentin in his study. Dick could hear his voice.

'Poor Aunt Fanny must be up too,' he thought. 'I can hear their voices. Oh, I'll soon fall asleep over my book. I'll slip down and out into the garden for a breath of fresh air That'll keep me awake.'

He put on his dressing gown and went quietly down the stairs. He undid the bolt of the garden door and slipped out. He stood listening for a moment, wondering if he'd hear the roar of the American's car in the stillness of the night.

But all he heard was the sound of the tyres of a bike on the road outside. A bike! Who was riding about at this time of night?

Dick stood in the shadows and watched. A man was on the bike. Dick could just make him out dimly, a big black shadow in the starlit night. To the boy's enormous surprise, he heard the sound of the man dismounting, then the swish of the leaves in the hedge as the bike was slung there.

Then someone came quietly up the path and went around to the window of the study. It was the only room in the house that was lit. Dick heard a tapping on the window, and then it was opened cautiously. His uncle's head appeared.

'Who is it?' he said, in a low tone. 'Is it you, Elbur?'

It apparently was. Dick saw that it was the big American who had visited his uncle two days before. 'I'll open the door,' said his aunt, but Elbur was already putting his leg across the windowsill!

Dick went back to bed, puzzled. How strange! Why should the American come so secretly in the night, why should he ride a bike instead of driving his car? He fell asleep still wondering.

He didn't know whether the American rode away again, or whether his aunt made a bed for him on a sofa downstairs. In fact, when he awoke the next morning, he wondered if it had all been a dream.

He asked his aunt, when he went down to breakfast.

'Did that man who phoned come last night?' he said.

His aunt nodded her head. 'Yes. But please say nothing about it. I don't want anyone to know. He's gone now.'

'Was it important?' asked Dick. 'Julian seemed to think it was, when he answered the phone.'

'Yes – it was important,' said Aunt Fanny. 'But not in the way you think. Don't ask me anything now, Dick. And keep out of your uncle's way. He's rather cross this morning.'

'Then something must have gone wrong with this new work he's doing,' thought Dick, and went to warn the others.

'It sounds exciting,' said Julian. 'I wonder what's up?'

They kept out of Uncle Quentin's way. They heard him grumbling loudly to his wife about something, they heard him slam his desk drawer as he always did when he was bad-tempered, and then he settled down to his morning's work.

Anne came running to the others after a while, looking surprised. 'George! I've just been into our room and guess what! Aunt Fanny's put a camp bed over in the corner – a camp bed made up with covers and everything! It's a real squash with two other beds as well in the room – mine and yours!'

'Someone else is coming to stay then – a girl,' said Dick. 'Or a woman. I expect it's a tutor to look after you and Anne, George, to see that you behave like little ladies!'

'Don't be silly,' said George, surprised and cross at the news. 'I'm going to ask Mum what it's all about. I won't have anyone else in our room. I just will *not*!'

But just as she was marching off to tell her mother this, the study door downstairs opened and her father bellowed into the hall, calling his wife.

'Fanny! Tell the children I want them. Tell them to come to my study AT ONCE!'

'Oh no – he does sound cross. What can we have done?' said Anne, scared.

## 3 Annoying news

The four children and Timmy trooped down the stairs together. George's mother was in the hall, just going to call them.

'Oh, there you are,' she said. 'I suppose you heard that you're wanted in the study. I'm coming too. And listen – *please* don't make any more fuss than you can help. I've had quite enough fuss made by Quentin!'

This was very mysterious! What had Aunt Fanny to do with whatever trouble there was? Into the study went the Five, Timmy too, and saw Uncle Quentin standing up looking as black as thunder.

'Quentin, *I* could have told the children,' began his wife, but he silenced her with a scowl exactly like the one George sometimes put on.

'I've got something to say to you,' he began. 'You remember those two friends of mine – scientists working on a scheme with me – you remember the big American?'

'Yes,' said everyone.

'He gave us some money,' said Anne.

Uncle Quentin took no notice of that remark. 'Well,' he said, 'he's got a daughter – let's see now – she's got some silly name . . .'

'Berta,' said his wife.

'Yes, Berta,' said Uncle Quentin. 'Well, Elbur, her dad, has been warned that she's going to be kidnapped.'

'What on earth for?' said Julian, amazed.

'Because it so happens that her dad knows more secrets about a new scheme we're planning than anyone else in the world,' said his uncle. 'And he says, quite frankly, that if this girl – what's her name now . . .'

'Berta,' said everyone, obligingly.

'That if this Berta is kidnapped, he'll give away every single secret he knows to get her back,' said Uncle Quentin. 'What's he made of? Traitor to us all! How can he even *think* of giving away secrets for the sake of a silly girl?'

'Quentin, she's his only child and he adores her,' said Aunt Fanny. 'I'd feel the same about George.'

'That's just soft and silly,' said her husband, in a tone of great disgust. 'It's a good thing *you* don't know any secrets – you'd give them away to the milkman!'

This was so ridiculous that the children laughed. Uncle Quentin glared at them.

'This is no laughing matter. It has been a great shock to me to be told by one of the leading scientists of the world that he feels certain he might give all our secrets to the enemy if this – this . . .'

'Berta,' said everyone again, at once.

'If this Berta was kidnapped,' went on Uncle Quentin. 'So he came to ask if we'd take this – this Berta into our own home for three weeks. By that time the scheme will be finished and launched, and our secrets will be safe.'

There was a silence. Nobody looked very pleased. In fact, George looked furious. She burst out at last.

'So *that's* who the bed is for in our room! Mum, have we *got* to be squashed up with nowhere to move around the room, for three whole weeks? It's not fair.'

'For once you and I agree, George,' said her

father. 'But I'm afraid you'll have to put up with it. Elbur is in such a state about this kidnapping warning that he couldn't be reasoned with. In fact he threatened to tear up all his figures and diagrams and burn them, if I didn't agree to this. That'd mean we couldn't get on with the scheme.'

'But why has she got to come *here*?' said George, fiercely. 'Why put her on to *us*? Hasn't she got any relations or friends she can go to?'

'George, don't be so fierce,' said her mother. 'Apparently Berta has no mother, and has been everywhere with her dad. They have no relations in this country – and no friends they can trust. He won't send her back to America because he's been warned by the police that she might be followed there – and at the moment he can't leave this country himself to go with her.'

'But why choose *us*?' said George again. 'He doesn't know a thing about us!'

'Well,' said her mother, with a small smile, 'when he met you all the other day he was apparently very impressed with you – and especially with *you*, George, although I can't imagine why. He said he'd rather his Berta was with you four than with any other family in the world.'

She paused and looked at the four, a harassed expression on her face. Julian went over to her.

'Don't worry!' he said. 'We'll look after Berta! I won't pretend I'm pleased at having a strange girl to join us these last three precious weeks – but I can see her dad's point of view – he's scared for Berta, and he's scared he might find himself spilling the beans if anything happened to her! It might be the only way he could get her back.'

'To think of such a thing!' burst out Uncle Quentin. 'All the work of the last two years! The man must be mad!'

'Now Quentin, don't think any more about it,' said his wife. 'I'm glad to have the child here. I'd hate George to be kidnapped, and I know exactly how he feels. You won't even notice she's here. One more will make no difference.'

'So you say,' grumbled her husband. 'Anyway, it's settled.'

'When is she coming?' asked Dick.

'Tonight. By boat,' said his uncle. 'We'll have to let Joanna the cook into the secret – but nobody else. That's understood, isn't it?'

'Of course,' said the four at once.

Then Uncle Quentin sat down firmly at his desk, and the children went hurriedly out of the room, Aunt Fanny behind them, and Timmy pushing between their ankles.

'It's such a pity, and I'm so sorry,' said Aunt Fanny. 'But I feel we can't do anything else.'

'I bet Timmy'll hate her,' said George.

'Don't you go and make things difficult, George,' said Julian. 'We're all agreed it can't be helped, so we might as well make the best of it.'

'I hate making the best of things,' said George, obstinately.

'Well,' said Dick, amiably, 'Julian and Anne and I could go back home and take Berta with us if you hate everything so much. I don't particularly want to stay here for three weeks if you're going to be in a mood all the time.'

'All right, I won't,' said George. 'I'm only letting off steam. You know that.'

'I'm never sure, with you,' said Dick, with a grin. 'Well, look – let's not spoil this one day when we *will* be by ourselves!'

They all tried valiantly to have as good a time as possible, and went out in George's boat for a long row to Lobster Cove. They didn't do any fishing there, but swam from the boat instead, in water as green and clear as in an open-air pool. Timmy didn't approve of swimming from boats. It was easy to jump out of the boat into the water – but he found it extremely difficult to jump in again!

Aunt Fanny had again packed them a wonderful lunch.

'An extra good one to make up for disappointment,' she said, smiling. Anne had given her a hug for that. They had all been making such a fuss about having someone extra – and Aunt Fanny had been the only one to feel real kindness for a child in danger.

They had enough food for tea too, and didn't get home until the evening. The sea was calm and blue, and the children could see almost to the bottom of the water, when they leaned over the side of the boat. The sky was the colour of harebells as they rowed into the bay and up to the beach.

'Will Berta be there yet, do you think?' said

George, mentioning the girl for the first time since they'd set out that morning.

'I shouldn't think so,' said Julian. 'Your dad said she'd be coming tonight – and I imagine that as she's coming by boat, it'll be dark – so that she won't be seen.'

'I expect she'll be feeling very scared,' said Anne. 'It must be horrible to be sent away to a strange place, to strange people. I'd hate it!'

They beached the boat and left it high and dry. Then they made their way to Kirrin Cottage. Aunt Fanny was pleased to see them.

'You're in good time for supper,' she said. 'Although if you ate everything I gave you today for your picnics, you'll probably find it difficult to eat very much supper.'

'Oh, I'm *starving*,' said Dick. He sniffed, holding his nose up in the air just as Timmy often did. 'I think you've been making your special tomato soup, Aunt Fanny!'

'You're too good at guessing,' said his aunt with a laugh. 'It was meant to be a surprise! Now go and wash and make yourselves tidy.'

'Berta hasn't come yet, I suppose, has she?' asked Julian.

'No,' said his aunt. 'And we'll have to think of another name for her, Julian. We can't call her Berta now.'

Uncle Quentin didn't appear for supper.

'He's having his in the study by himself,' said Aunt Fanny.

There was a sigh of relief. Nobody had looked forward to seeing Uncle Quentin that night. It took him quite a long time to get over any annoyance!

'How sunburnt you all are!' said Aunt Fanny, looking around the table. 'George, your nose is beginning to peel.'

'I know,' said George. 'I wish it didn't. Anne's never does. Oh, I'm sleepy!'

'Well, go to bed as soon as you've finished your supper,' said her mother.

'I'd like to. But what about this Berta?' said George. 'What time is she coming? It'd be a bit mean to be in bed when she arrives.'

'I've no idea what time she'll come,' said her mother. 'But I'll wait up, of course. There's no need for anyone else to. I expect she'll be tired and scared, so I'll give her something to eat – some of the tomato soup, if you've left any! – and then pop her into bed. I expect she'd be glad not to have to meet any of you tonight.'

'Well – *I'll* go to bed,' said Dick. 'I heard Mr Elbur arriving last night, Aunt Fanny, and it was pretty late, wasn't it? I can hardly keep my eyes open tonight.'

'Come on, then – let's all go up,' said Julian. 'We can read if we can't sleep. Good night, Aunt Fanny. Thank you for that lovely picnic food again!'

All the four went upstairs, Anne and Dick yawning loudly, and setting the others off too. Timmy padded behind them, glad that George was going to bed so early.

They were all asleep in ten minutes. The boys slept like logs and didn't stir at all. The girls fell fast asleep for about four hours – and then George was woken by hearing Timmy growl. She sat up at once.

'What is it?' she said. 'Oh – is it Berta arriving, Tim? Let's keep quiet and see what she's like!'

After a minute Timmy growled again. George heard the sound of quiet footsteps on the stairs. Then the bedroom door was slid softly open, and two people stood in the light from the landing. One was Aunt Fanny.

The other, of course, was Berta.

## 4 Berta

George sat up in bed and stared at Berta. She looked very strange indeed. For one thing she was so wrapped up in coats and scarves that it was difficult to see if she was fat or thin, tall or short, and for another thing she was crying so bitterly that her face was all screwed up.

Anne didn't wake up. Timmy was so astonished that, like George, he just sat and stared.

'Tell Timmy not to make a sound,' whispered George's mother, afraid that the dog might bark the house down, once he began.

George laid a warning hand on Timmy. Her mother gave Berta a little push farther into the room.

'She's been very seasick, poor child,' she told George. 'And she's scared and upset. I want her to get into bed as soon as possible.'

Berta was still sobbing, but the sobs grew quieter as she began to feel less sick. George's mother was so kind and sensible that she felt comforted.

'Let's take these things off,' she said to Berta. 'You *are* wrapped up! But if you came in an open motorboat I expect you needed them.'

'What should I call you?' asked Berta, with one last sniff.

'You'd better call me Aunt Fanny, as the others do, I think,' said George's mother. 'I expect you know why you've come to stay with us for a while, don't you?'

'Yes,' said Berta. 'I didn't want to come. I wanted to stay with my dad. I'm not afraid of being kidnapped. I've got Sally to look after me.'

'Who's Sally, dear?' asked Aunt Fanny, taking a coat or two off Berta.

'My dog,' said Berta. 'She's downstairs in the basket I was carrying.'

George pricked up her ears at *that* bit of news!

'A dog!' she said. 'We can't have a dog here. Mine would never allow that. Would you, Timmy?'

Timmy gave a small wuff. He was watching this night arrival with great interest. Who was she? He was longing to get down from George's bed and go to sniff at her, but George had her hand on his collar.

'Well, I've brought my dog, and I just reckon she'll have to stay now,' said Berta. 'The boat's gone back. Anyway, I wouldn't go anywhere without Sally. I told my dad that, and he said all right then, take her with you! So I did.'

'Mum, tell her how fierce Timmy is and that he'd fight any other dog who came here,' said George, urgently. 'I won't have anybody else's dog at Kirrin Cottage.'

To George's annoyance her mother took not the slightest notice. She went on helping Berta take off scarves, thick socks and goodness knows what. George wondered how anyone could possibly exist in all those clothes on a warm summer's night.

At last Berta stood in a simple jumper and skirt, a slim, pretty little girl with large blue eyes and wavy golden hair. She shook back her hair and rubbed her face with a hanky.

'Thank you,' she said. 'Can I get Sally now?'

'Not tonight,' said Aunt Fanny. 'You see, you're going to sleep in that little camp bed over in the corner – and I can't let you have your dog here too, because she and Timmy might fight unless we introduce them to one another properly. And there's no time to bother about that tonight. Do you feel hungry now? Would you like some tomato soup and biscuits?'

'Yes, please. I do feel a bit hungry,' said Berta. 'I've been so sick on that awful bumpy boat that I don't expect there's anything left inside me at all!'

'Well, look – you unpack your bag, and have a wash in the bathroom if you want to, and then get into your pyjamas,' said Aunt Fanny. 'Then hop into bed and I'll bring you up some soup.'

But one look at the scowling George made her change her mind. Better not leave poor Berta with an angry George on her very first night!

'I think perhaps I won't get the soup myself,' she said. 'George, you go and get it, will you? It's warming up in the saucepan on the stove downstairs. You'll see the little soup cup on the table, and some biscuits too.'

George got out of bed, still looking very mutinous. She watched Berta shake out a nightie from her bag and pursed up her lips.

'She doesn't even wear pyjamas!' she thought.

'What a baby! And she's had the nerve to bring her own dog, too – spoilt little thing! I wonder where it is? I think I'll have a look at it when I'm downstairs.'

But her mother had an idea that George might do that and she went to the door after her.

'George!' she said, warningly, 'I don't want you to open the dog's basket downstairs. I'm not having any dogfights tonight. I'll put him in Timmy's kennel outside before I go to bed.'

George said nothing but went on downstairs. The soup was just about to boil and she whipped it off the stove at once. She poured it into the little soup cup, placed it on the saucer, and put some biscuits on the side.

She heard a small whimpering sound, and turned around. It came from a fairly large basket over in the corner. George was tempted to go and undo it – but she knew that if the new dog ran upstairs to find its mistress, Timmy would bark and wake everybody up! It wasn't worth risking.

She took up the soup. Berta was now in the camp bed and looked very cosy. Anne was still sleeping peacefully, completely undisturbed by all that was going on. Timmy had taken the opportunity of jumping off George's bed and had gone to examine this newcomer. He sniffed her delicately, and Berta put out her hand and stroked his head.

'What lovely eyes he's got,' she said. 'But he's a mongrel, isn't he? A sort of mixture-dog.'

'Don't you say anything like that to George,' said Aunt Fanny. 'She adores Timmy. Now – do you feel better? I hope you'll be happy with us, Berta – I'm sure you didn't want to come – but your dad was so worried. And it'll be nice for you to get to know Anne and Georgina before you go to their school next term.'

'Oh – was that Georgina – the one you called George?' said Berta in surprise. 'I wasn't really sure if she was a boy or not. My dad told me there were three boys here and one girl – and that's the girl, isn't it – in bed there?'

She pointed to Anne. Aunt Fanny nodded. 'Yes, that's Anne. Your dad thought George was a boy, that's why he told you there were three boys and only one girl here, I suppose. The two boys are in the next room.'

'I don't like George very much,' said Berta. 'She doesn't want me here, does she – or my dog?'

'Oh, you'll find George great fun when you get to know her,' said Aunt Fanny. 'Here she comes now with your soup.'

George came in with the soup, and wasn't at all pleased to see Timmy standing by the camp bed, being petted by Berta. She set the soup down sharply and pushed Timmy away.

'Thank you,' said Berta, and took the soup cup eagerly into her hands. 'What *lovely* soup!' she said.

George got into bed and turned over on her side. She knew she was behaving badly, but the thought of someone daring to bring another *dog* to live at Kirrin Cottage was more than she could bear.

Timmy leapt up to lie at her feet as usual. Berta looked at this with much approval.

'I'll have Sally on *my* feet tomorrow!' she said. 'That's a really good idea. Pops – that's my dad – always let me have Sally in my room, but she had to be in her basket, not on my bed. Tomorrow night she can sleep on my feet, like Timmy does on George's.'

'She will not,' said George, in a fierce voice. 'No dog sleeps in my bedroom except Timmy.'

'Now don't talk any more,' said Aunt Fanny, hurriedly. 'We can settle everything tomorrow when you're not so tired. I'll look after Sally tonight for you, I promise. Lie down now and go to sleep. You look as if you're half asleep already!'

Berta was suddenly overcome with sleep and flopped down into bed. Her eyes closed, but she managed to force them open and look up at George's mother.

'Good night, Aunt Fanny,' she said, sleepily. 'That's what I was supposed to call you, wasn't it? Thank you for being so kind to me.'

She was asleep almost before she'd finished speaking. Aunt Fanny picked up the soup cup and went to the door. 'Are you awake, George?' she said.

George lay absolutely still. She knew that her mother wasn't pleased with her. It'd be better to pretend to be fast asleep!

'I'm sure you're awake,' said her mother. 'And I hope you're ashamed of yourself. I'll expect you to make up for this silly behaviour in the morning. It's a pity to behave in such a childish manner!'

She went out of the room, closing the door

softly. George put out her hand to Timmy. She was ashamed of herself, but she wasn't at all certain that she'd behave better in the morning. That silly, soppy girl! Her dog would be as silly as herself, she was sure! And Timmy would *hate* having another dog in the house. He'd probably growl and snarl so much that Berta would be forced to send her dog away.

'And a good thing too,' murmured George, as Timmy licked her fingers lovingly. '*You* don't want another girl in the house or another dog either, do you, Timmy? Especially a girl like that!'

Aunt Fanny saw to Berta's dog, and put her safely into Timmy's kennel outside. It had a little door to it, which could be shut, so the dog was safe there, and wouldn't be able to run out.

She went back into the house, cleared up Berta's belongings a little, for they had been thrown higgledy-piggledy into the room, and then turned out the light.

She went upstairs to bed. Her husband had slept soundly all through Berta's late arrival. He'd been very sure that he'd wake up and welcome the girl as well as his wife, but he hadn't even stirred!

Aunt Fanny was glad. It was much easier for her to deal with a seasick, frightened girl by herself. She climbed thankfully into bed and lay down with a sigh. 'Oh dear – I'm not looking forward to the morning! What will happen then, with George in this mood, and two dogs to sort out? Berta seems a nice little thing. Well – perhaps they'll all get on better than I think!'

Yes – things wouldn't be too easy in the morning, that was for sure!

## 5 In the morning

George was the first to wake up in the morning. She at once remembered the events of the night before and looked across at Berta in the camp bed. The girl was asleep, her wavy golden hair spread over the pillow. George leaned across Anne's bed and gave her a sharp nudge.

Anne woke up at once and gazed sleepily at George. 'What's the matter, George? Is it time to get up?'

'Look over there,' whispered George, nodding her head towards Berta. Anne turned over and looked. Unlike George she liked the look of Berta. Her sleeping face was pleasant and open, and her mouth turned up, not down. Anne couldn't bear people whose mouths turned down.

'She looks all right,' whispered back Anne.

George frowned.

'She howled like anything when she came,'

she told Anne. 'She's a real baby. And she's brought a dog!'

'Timmy won't like that,' said Anne, startled. 'Where is it?'

'Down in Timmy's kennel,' said George, still whispering. 'I haven't seen it. It was in a closed basket last night and I didn't dare open it in case it ran upstairs and had a fight with Tim. But it can't be very big. I expect it's a horrible Peke, or some silly little lapdog.'

'Pekes aren't horrible,' said Anne. 'They may be small and have funny little pug noses, but they're really brave. Imagine having another dog! I wonder what Timmy will say!'

'It's a pity Berta isn't like us,' said George. 'Look at her pale face – no suntan! And she looks *weedy*, doesn't she? I bet she couldn't climb a tree or row a boat, or . . .'

'Shh! She's waking up,' said Anne warningly.

Berta yawned and stretched herself. Then she opened her eyes and looked around. At first she had no idea where she was, and then she suddenly remembered. She sat up.

'Hello!' said Anne, and smiled at her. 'You weren't there when I came to bed last night. I was surprised to see you this morning.'

Berta took an immediate liking to Anne. She's got kind eyes, she thought. She's not like the other girl. I like this one!

She smiled back at Anne.

'Yes – I came in the middle of the night,' she said. 'I came by motorboat and the sea was so bumpy that I was really sick. My dad didn't come with me but a friend of his did and he had to carry me from the boat to Kirrin Cottage. Even my legs felt seasick!'

'Poor you!' said Anne. 'You didn't really enjoy the adventure then!'

'No. I can do without adventures!' said Berta. 'I'm not keen on them. Especially when Pops gets all excited and worried about me – he fusses around me like a hen. I'll hate being away from him.'

George was listening to all this. Not keen on adventures! Well, a girl like that wouldn't be, of course!

'*I'm* not very keen on adventures either,' said Anne. 'We've had lots. I prefer adventures when they're all over!'

George exploded. 'Anne! How can you talk

like that? We've had some *fantastic* adventures, and we've enjoyed every one of them. If you feel like that we'll leave you out of the next one.'

Anne laughed. 'You won't! An adventure comes up all of a sudden, like a wind blowing up in the sky, and we're all in it, whether we like it or not. And you know that I like sharing things with you. Hey – isn't it time we got up?'

'Yes,' said George, looking at the clock on the mantelpiece. 'Unless Berta wants to have her breakfast in bed? I bet she always does at home.'

'No, I don't. I hate meals in bed,' said Berta. 'I'm going to get up.'

She leapt out of bed and went to the window. Immediately she saw the wide sweep of the bay, sparkling in the morning sun, as blue as cornflowers. The sea-sparkle was reflected into the bedroom, and made it very bright indeed.

'Oh. I *wondered* why our room was so full of light,' said Berta. 'Now I know! What a view! Oh, how lovely the sea looks this morning! And what's that little island out there? What a lovely place it looks.'

'That's Kirrin Island,' said George, proudly. 'It belongs to *me*.'

Berta laughed, thinking that George was joking. 'Belongs to *you*! I bet you wish it did. It's really wunnerful!'

'*Wunnerful*!' said George imitating her. 'Can't you say "wonderful"? It's got a D in the middle, you know.'

'Yes. I'm always being told things like that,' said Berta, still staring out of the window. 'I had an English tutor and she tried to make me speak like you do. I try, because I've got to go to an English school. I wish that island belonged to *me*. I wonder if Pops could buy it.'

George exploded again. '*Buy* it! You idiot, I *told* you it was mine, didn't I?'

Berta turned around in surprise. 'But – you didn't *mean* it, did you?' she said. '*Yours*? How could it be?'

'It *is* George's,' said Anne. 'It has always belonged to the Kirrin family. That's Kirrin Island. George's dad gave it to her, after an adventure we once had.'

Berta stared at George in awe. 'Great snakes! So it *is* yours! Aren't you lucky! Will you take me to visit it?'

'I'll see,' said George gruffly, glad to have

impressed this American girl so much. Getting her 'Pops' to buy the island indeed! George snorted to herself. What next?

A shout came from the next room. It was Julian. 'Hey, you girls! Are you getting up? We're all too late for a swim before breakfast this morning. Dick and I have only just woken up.'

'Berta's here!' shouted back Anne. 'We'll get dressed, all of us, and then we'll introduce Berta to you.'

'Are they your brothers?' asked Berta. 'I haven't got any. Or sisters either. I'll be pretty scared of them.'

'You won't be scared of Julian and Dick,' said Anne, proudly. 'You'll wish you had brothers like them. Won't she, George?'

'Yes,' said George, shortly. She was feeling rather annoyed just then because Timmy was standing by Berta, wagging his plumy tail. 'Come here, Timmy. Don't make a nuisance of yourself.'

'Oh, he's not,' said Berta, and patted his big head. 'I like him. He seems absolutely ENORMOUS after my Sally. But you'll love Sally, George, you really will. Everyone says how sweet she is – and I've trained her beautifully.'

George took no interest in these remarks at all. She flounced off to wash in the bathroom, but Julian and Dick were there, and there was a lot of yelling and shouting as George tried to make them hurry up and get out. Berta laughed.

'That sounds nice and family-like,' she said. 'You don't get that sort of thing if you're an only child. What do I wear here?'

'Oh – something very simple,' said Anne, looking at the suitcase open on the floor, showing a collection of Berta's clothes. 'That shirt and those jeans will do.'

They were ready just as the gong rang for breakfast. A delicious smell of frying bacon and tomatoes came up the stairs, and Berta sniffed in delight.

'I do like English breakfast,' she said. 'We haven't gotten around to a proper breakfast in America yet! That's bacon and tomatoes I smell, isn't it? My English tutor always said that bacon and eggs made the best breakfast in the world, but I guess the one we're going to have will taste pretty good.'

Uncle Quentin was at the table when the

children came down. He looked very surprised to see Berta, having completely forgotten that she was coming.

'Who's this?' he said.

'Now Quentin – don't pretend you don't know!' said his wife. 'It's Elbur's girl – your friend Elbur. She came in the middle of the night, but I didn't wake you, you were so sound asleep.'

'Ah yes,' said Uncle Quentin, and he shook hands with the rather scared Berta. 'Glad to have you here, er – let me see now – what's your name?'

'Berta,' said everyone in a chorus.

'Yes, yes – Berta. Sit down, my dear. I know your dad well. He's doing some wonderful work.'

Berta beamed. 'He's always at work!' she said. 'He works all through the night sometimes.'

'Does he? What a thing to do!' said Uncle Quentin.

'It's a thing you often do yourself, Quentin,' said his wife, pouring out coffee. 'Though I don't suppose you even realise it.'

Uncle Quentin looked surprised. 'Do I really? Don't I go to bed some nights then?'

Berta laughed. 'You're like my Pops! Sometimes

he doesn't know what day of the week it is, even! And yet he's supposed to be one of the cleverest guys in the world!'

But Uncle Quentin wasn't listening. He'd suddenly seen a letter marked 'IMPORTANT' on the top of his pile of correspondence, and he picked it up.

'Well, unless I'm much mistaken, here's a letter from your dad,' he said to Berta. 'I'll see what it says.'

He opened the letter and read it to himself. Then he looked up. 'It's all about you – er . . .'

'Her name's Berta,' said Aunt Fanny, patiently.

'About you, Berta,' said Uncle Quentin. 'But your dad has some very strange ideas. Yes, very strange.'

'What are they?' asked his wife.

'Well – he says she must be disguised – in case anyone comes to find her here,' said Uncle Quentin. 'And he wants her name changed – and he wants us to buy her boys' clothes – and cut her hair short – and dress her up as a boy!'

Everyone listened in surprise. Berta gave a little squeal.

'I won't! I WON'T be dressed up as a boy! I

*won't* have my hair cut off. Don't you dare to make me! I WON'T!'

## 6 A *few upsets*

Berta looked so upset that Aunt Fanny acted quickly and firmly. 'Don't bother about that letter now, Quentin,' she said. 'We'll go through it afterwards and decide what to do. Let's have our breakfast in peace.'

'I *won't* have my hair cut off,' said Berta, again.

Uncle Quentin wasn't used to being defied openly like this, and he scowled. He looked at his wife.

'Surely you're not going to let this – er what's her name now – Bertha . . .'

'Berta,' said everyone automatically.

'I said that we wouldn't discuss this till after breakfast,' said Aunt Fanny, in the kind of voice that made everyone, including Uncle Quentin, sure that she meant what she said. Her husband folded up the letter and opened the next one, frowning. The children looked at one another.

Berta to be a boy! If ever anyone looked less like a boy it was Berta! George was very annoyed. She loved to dress like a boy, but she didn't feel inclined to urge anyone else to! She looked at Berta, who was eating her breakfast with tears in her eyes. What a baby! She wouldn't even *look* like a boy, if she was dressed in boys' clothes. She'd just look absolutely ridiculous.

Julian began a conversation with his aunt about the garden. She was grateful to him for breaking up the sudden awkwardness caused by the letter. She was very fond of Julian. 'I can always depend on him,' she thought, and talked gladly of the garden fruit, and who'd pick the raspberries for lunch and whether the wasps would eat *all* the plums or not!

Dick joined in, and Anne, and soon Berta did too. Only George and her father remained gloomy. They both looked so exactly alike with solemn, rather frowning expressions that Julian nudged Dick and nodded towards them.

Dick grinned. 'Like father, like daughter!' he said. 'Cheer up, George. Don't you like your breakfast?'

George was just about to answer crossly when

Anne gave an exclamation. 'Oh, *look* at Uncle Quentin! He's putting mustard on his toast – Aunt Fanny, stop him – he's just going to eat it!'

Everyone roared with laughter. Aunt Fanny managed to smack her husband's hand down from his mouth, just as he was putting his toast and mustard up to it, reading a letter at the same time.

'Hey – what's the matter?' he said, startled.

'*Quentin* – that's the second time this month you've spread your toast with mustard instead of marmalade,' said his wife. 'Please have a little sense.'

After that everyone became very cheerful. Uncle Quentin laughed at himself, and George saw the funny side and laughed loudly too, which made Timmy bark, and Berta giggled. Aunt Fanny was quite relieved that her husband had done such a silly thing.

'Do you remember when Dad poured custard all over his fried fish once?' George said, entering into the talk for the first time. 'And he said it was the best egg sauce he'd ever tasted?'

The conversation was very animated after that, and Aunt Fanny felt happier.

'You children can clear away and wash up the breakfast things for Joanna,' she said. 'Or two of you can and the others can make the beds with me.'

'What about my little dog?' said Berta, suddenly remembering her again. 'I haven't seen her yet, because I was only just in time for breakfast. Where is she?'

'You can go and get her now,' said Aunt Fanny. 'We've all finished. Are you going to start your work, Quentin?'

'Yes, I am,' said her husband. 'So I don't want any yelling or shouting or barking outside my study door.'

He got up and went out of the room. Berta stood up too.

'Where's the kennel?' she said.

'I'll show you,' said Anne. 'We'll go and get your dog and introduce it to Timmy. Coming, George?'

'You can bring the dog in here, and we'll see what Timmy says,' said George, going all gloomy again. 'If he doesn't like the dog – and he won't – it'll have to live out in the kennel.'

'Oh *no*,' said Berta, at once.

'Well, you don't want Timmy to *eat* it, do you?' said George. 'He's very jealous of other dogs in the house. He might go for yours and savage it.'

'Oh *no*!' said Berta, again, looking upset. 'Timmy's nice. He's not a fierce dog.'

'That's all *you* know!' said George. 'Well, I've warned you.'

'Come on,' said Anne, pulling at Berta's sleeve. 'Let's go and fetch Sally. She must be wondering why nobody's been to see her. I bet Timmy won't mind *very* much.'

As soon as the two had gone out, George spoke in Timmy's ear. 'You don't like strange dogs who want to come and live here, do you, Tim? You'll growl and snarl like anything, won't you? Growl your very fiercest! I know you won't bite but if you could just growl your loudest, that'll be enough. Berta will make that Sally-dog live out of doors then!'

Soon she heard footsteps returning, and Anne's voice exclaiming in delight.

'Oh, she's sweet! Oh, what a darling! Sally, you're a pet! Julian, Dick, Aunt Fanny – come and see Berta's dog!'

Everyone came into the room, led by Berta and

Anne. Berta held the dog in her arms.

It was a tiny black poodle, whose woolly fur was cut away here and there to give it a very funny look. Sally was certainly an attractive little thing! Her sharp little nose sniffed all the time she was carried into the room, and her quick little eyes looked everywhere.

Berta put her down, and the little poodle stood there, poised on her dainty feet like a ballet dancer about to perform. Everyone but George exclaimed in delight.

'She's a poppet!'

'Sally! Sally, you're a pet!'

'Oh, a poodle! I love poodles! They look so knowing.'

Timmy stood by George, sniffing hard to get the smell of this new dog. George had her hand on his collar in case he sprang. His tail was as stiff as a ramrod.

The poodle suddenly saw him. She stared at him out of bright little eyes, completely unafraid. Then she pulled away from Berta's hand and trotted right over to Timmy, her funny little tail wagging merrily.

Timmy backed away a little in surprise. The

poodle danced all around him on her toes, and gave a little whimpering bark, which said as clearly as possible, I want to play with you!

Timmy sprang. He leapt in the air and came down with a thud on his big paws, and the little poodle dodged. Timmy's tail began to wag wildly. He sprang again in play, and almost knocked the little poodle over. He barked as if to say 'Sorry, I didn't mean that!'

Then he and the poodle played a ridiculous game of dodge and run, and although one or two chairs went flying nobody minded – they were all laughing so much at the sight of the quick little poodle leading Timmy such a dance.

At last Sally was tired and sat down in a corner. Timmy pranced about in front of her, showing off. Then he went up to her and sniffed her nose. He licked it gently, and then lay down in front of her, gazing at her adoringly.

Anne gave a little squeal of laughter.

'He's gazing at Sally exactly as he gazes at you, George!' she cried.

But George wasn't at all pleased. In fact she was completely astounded. To think that Timmy should *welcome* another dog! To think that he should behave like this when she had told him to do the opposite!

'Aren't they sweet together?' said Berta, pleased. 'I *thought* Timmy would like Sally. Of course Sally is a pedigree dog, and cost a lot of money – and Timmy's only a mongrel. I expect he thinks she's *wunnerful.*'

'Oh, Tim may be a mongrel, but he's absolutely wunnerful too,' said Dick, hastily, pronouncing the word like Berta, to try and get a laugh. He saw George's scowl, and knew how cross she felt at hearing her beloved Timmy compared with a pedigree dog.

'He's a fantastic dog, aren't you, Timmy?' went on Dick. 'Sally may be sweet, but you're worth more than a *hundred* sweet dogs, aren't you?'

'I think he's beautiful,' said Berta, looking down at Timmy. 'He's got the loveliest eyes I ever saw.'

George began to feel a little better. She called Timmy.

'You're making a fool of yourself,' she said to him.

'Now that Timmy and Sally are going to be friends, can I have Sally to sleep on my bed at night, like George has Timmy?' said Berta. 'Please say yes, Aunt Fanny.'

'No,' said George at once. 'Mum, I won't have that. I won't!'

'Well, we'll see what we can do about it,' said her mother. 'Sally was quite happy in the kennel last night.'

'I'm going to have her sleep with me,' said Berta, scowling at George. 'My dad will pay you a lot of money to make me happy. He told me he would.'

'Don't be silly, Berta,' said Aunt Fanny, firmly. 'This isn't a question of money. Now, leave this for a little while, please, and go and do your jobs, all of you. And then we must think about your dad's letter, Berta, and see exactly what he wants done. We must certainly try to follow his advice about you.'

'But I don't want to—' began Berta, and then felt a firm hand on her arm. It was Julian.

'Come on, kid,' he said. 'Act your age! Remember you're a guest here and put on a few of your best manners. We like American children – but not *spoilt* ones!'

Berta was shocked to hear Julian speaking like

this. She looked up at him and he grinned down at her. She felt near tears, but she smiled back.

'You haven't got any brothers,' said Julian, linking his arm in hers. 'Well, from now on, while you're here, Dick and I are your brothers. What do you think?'

Berta felt that there was nothing in the world she'd like better than having Julian for a brother! He was big and tall and had twinkling kindly eyes that made Berta feel he was as responsible and trustable as her father.

Aunt Fanny smiled to herself. Julian always knew the best thing to say and do. Now he'd take Berta in hand and see that she didn't upset the household too much. She was glad. It wasn't easy to run a big family like this, with a scientist husband to cope with, unless everyone helped out!

'You go and help Aunt Fanny with the beds,' said Julian to Berta. 'And take your Sally-dog with you. She's great! But so is Timmy, and don't you forget it!'

## 7  A little conference

Peace reigned in the house for a little while. Dick and Julian cleared away, and George and Anne went to help the cook with the washing up. Joanna was pleased, because with eight people in the house, including herself, there was a lot to do.

She had been very astonished that morning to find a fifth child added to the household, but had been told that after breakfast she could go into the sitting room and hear an explanation! Joanna had to be in on the secret too!

Upstairs Berta was helping with the beds – not very successfully because she wasn't used to doing things for herself. But she was very willing to learn and Aunt Fanny was quite pleased with her. Timmy and Sally darted about together and made things more difficult than they need have been, popping under beds and out again at top speed.

'I'm glad Timmy likes Sally,' said Berta. 'I knew he would. I don't know why George thought he wouldn't. George is funny, I think.'

'Not really,' said Aunt Fanny. 'She hasn't had any brothers or sisters to rub off her corners, and she didn't even know her three cousins till a few years ago, or go to school. Lonely people aren't as easy to get on with as others – but she's great fun now, as you'll soon find out.'

'I'm an only child too,' said Berta. 'But I've always had plenty of other children to play with. My Pop saw to that. He's wunnerful – I mean wonDERful. I'll say that word "wonDERful" twenny times, then maybe I'll get it right.'

'Well, say the word "twenty" as well!' said Aunt Fanny. 'It has a letter T at the end as well as at the beginning, you know. It's "twenTY" not "twenny". But don't make yourself *too* English. It's nice to have a change!'

'WonDERful, wonDERful, wonDERful! TwenTY, twenTY!' chanted Berta, as she made the beds. Dick looked into the room and chuckled.

'Great snakes!' he said, with a grin, and an American accent. 'You shore are wunnerful, baby!'

'Don't be so silly, Dick,' said his aunt, laughing.

'Now – I think we've finished all we have to do, Berta. We'll go downstairs and have a conference. Tell the others, will you?'

Berta, followed closely by Sally, who was also followed closely by an adoring Timmy, went to tell Dick and Julian, and then George and Anne. George wasn't too pleased with Timmy.

'Where have you been?' she said. 'Can't you stop running about after Sally? She'll get very very tired of you!'

'Wuff!' said Sally, in a high little bark, not at all like Timmy's deep 'Woof!'

Soon all five children and the two dogs, and also Joanna, were in the sitting room with Aunt Fanny. Berta began to look a bit nervous.

Aunt Fanny had the letter that Berta's father had sent. She didn't read it out to the children, but told them what was in it. She also explained to Joanna about Berta.

'Joanna, you've always known what important work my husband does,' she said. 'Well, Berta's dad does the same kind of work in America, and he and Quentin are working on a great new scheme together.'

'Oh yes,' said Joanna, very much interested.

'Berta's dad has been warned by the police that it's possible Berta may be kidnapped and held to ransom, not for money, but for the scientific secrets that he knows,' went on Aunt Fanny. 'So she's been sent to us to be kept safe for three weeks. By that time the scheme will be finished and made public. Berta is going to the same school as Anne and George, and it's a good idea to let them know one another first.'

Joanna nodded. 'I understand that,' she said. 'I think we can keep Berta safe, don't you?'

'Yes,' said Aunt Fanny. 'But her dad has now put up some further ideas that he wants us to follow. He says it'd be best to disguise her as a boy—'

'Good idea,' interrupted Dick.

'And to give her another name – a boy's name,' said Aunt Fanny. 'He wants her to have her hair cut short and—'

'Oh please not that!' begged Berta, shaking back her fair, wavy hair. 'I'd hate it. Girls with short hair like boys look so silly, they—'

Anne nudged her and frowned. Berta stopped hurriedly, remembering that George had curly hair cut as short as any boy.

'I think we'll have to do what your dad says,' said Aunt Fanny. 'This is very important, Berta. You see, if anyone *should* come here looking for you, thinking of kidnapping, they'd never recognise you if you were looking exactly like a boy.'

'But my hair,' said Berta, almost in tears. 'How *could* Pops say I have to have my hair off? He always said it was wunnerful!'

Nobody liked to point out that there was a D in wonderful just then! Berta was really upset about her hair.

'Your hair will grow quickly enough,' said Aunt Fanny.

'Her *head's* a good shape,' said Julian, looking at it consideringly. 'She should look nice with short hair.'

Berta cheered up. If Julian thought that, then it wouldn't be so bad.

'But what about clothes?' she said, remembering this point with a look of horror. 'Girls look silly in boys' clothes.'

'You won't look any worse than George does,' said Dick. 'She's got on a boy's jumper, boy's jeans and boy's shoes right now!'

'I think she looks silly,' said Berta, obstinately, and George scowled.

'Well, I think *you*'d look horrible,' she said. 'You wouldn't even *look* like a boy, you'd look little-girlish. *I* think it's a stupid idea to put you into boys' clothes!'

'Aha! Our George wants to be the only one!' said Dick, slyly, and quickly got out of the way of a shove from the furious George.

'Well,' said Julian. 'I'll go out and buy some things for Berta this morning, so that's settled. What about her hair? Shall *I* cut it short?'

Aunt Fanny was amused at Julian's take-charge way of dealing with Berta and her troubles, and even more amused to see that Berta didn't even argue with Julian.

'You can certainly go shopping for Berta if you like,' she said. 'But I'd rather you didn't cut her hair. You'd make her look a scarecrow!'

'I don't mind if Julian cuts it,' said Berta, surprisingly meek all at once.

'I'll cut it for you myself,' said Aunt Fanny. 'Now – what about a boy's name? We can't call you Berta any more, that's for sure.'

'I'd rather not have a boy's name,' said Berta.

'It's silly for a girl to be called by a boy's name, like George.'

'If you *mean* to be rude to me, I'll—' began George, but got no farther. Julian and Dick had burst into laughter.

'Oh George – you and Berta will be the death of us!' said Julian. 'Here are you doing all you can to *pretend* to be a boy – and here's Berta doing all she can to get *out* of it! For goodness' sake, let's decide without any more bickering. We'll call Berta Robert.'

'No – that's too like Berta,' said Dick. 'It ought to be a completely different name. Let's call her an ordinary boy's name like Jim or Tom or John.'

'No,' said Berta. 'I don't like any of them. Let me have my second name, please.'

'What's that? Another girl's name?' asked Julian.

'Yes. But it's used for a boy too, only then it's spelt differently,' said Berta. 'It's Lesley. It's a nice name, I think.'

'Lesley. Yes – it suits you,' said Julian. 'It suits you better than Berta. We'll call you Lesley – and people will think it's Leslie spelt l-i-e at the end, and not l-e-y. All right. Everything's settled.'

'Not quite,' said his aunt. 'I just want to say that you mustn't let Berta – I mean Lesley – out of your sight at all. And you must report at once any mysterious happening or any stranger you see. The local police here know that we have Lesley with us, and why – and anything can be reported to them at once. They're also keeping a good lookout, of course.'

'This almost sounds as if we're in the middle of an adventure!' said Dick, looking pleased.

'I hope not,' said his aunt. 'I don't imagine that anyone will ever guess Berta – I mean Lesley – is anything more than she'll seem to be – a male friend of yours and Julian's, come to stay for a while. It's going to be difficult to refer to her as him all the time!'

'It certainly is,' said Julian, standing up. 'If you'll give me some money, Aunt Fanny, I'll go and do a bit of shopping for Lesley. What size do you think HE needs?'

Everyone laughed. 'HE wears size three shoes,' said Joanna smiling. 'I noticed that this morning.'

'And HE will have to get used to doing his coat

buttons up on the right-hand side instead of on the left,' said Anne, joining in the fun.

'SHE will soon get used to that,' said George. 'Won't SHE, Timmy?'

'Don't spoil it all now, George,' said Julian. 'A slip of the tongue, saying SHE instead of HE, might lead to danger for Ber – I mean Lesley.'

'Yes, I know,' said George. 'It's just that she'll never look like a boy, and—'

'I don't *want* to look like a boy,' said Berta. 'I think *you* look—'

'Here we go again!' said Julian. 'Stop it, Lesley, stop it, George. George, you'd better come out and help me to get the things for Lesley. Come on. And take that scowl off your face. You look like a sulky girl!'

That made George alter her face at once. She couldn't help grinning at Julian.

'I'm coming,' she said. 'Goodbye, Berta. When we come back, you'll be Lesley, haircut and all!'

She and Julian went off. Anne fetched her aunt's sharpest scissors and draped a big towel around Berta's shoulders. Berta looked as if she was going to cry.

'Cheer up,' said Dick. 'You're going to look

angelic with short hair! Go on, Aunt Fanny. Let's see what she's like with shorn locks.'

'Sit still,' said Aunt Fanny and began.

Clip-clip-clip! The wavy golden hair fell to the floor in big strands and Berta began to weep in earnest. 'My hair! I can't bear this. Oh, my hair!'

Soon most of it was on the floor, and Aunt Fanny began to clip what was left as best she could, to make it look as boyish as possible. She made a very good job of it indeed. Dick and Anne watched with the greatest interest.

'There! It's done!' said Aunt Fanny at last. 'Stop crying, Lesley – and let's have a look at you!'

## 8  A transformation

Berta stood in the middle of the floor, blinking her tears away. Anne gave a gasp.

'You know – it's *very* odd – but she does look like a boy – a very, very good-looking boy!'

'An angelic boy,' said Dick. 'A choirboy or something. She looks fantastic! Who'd have thought it?'

Aunt Fanny was very struck with Berta's appearance too.

'It's certainly very odd,' she said. 'But there's no doubt about it – when she's – I mean he's – dressed in boys' clothes, he'll make a very convincing boy. Better than George, actually, because her hair's *really* too curly for a boy.'

Berta went to the mirror on the wall. She gave a wail. 'I took awful! I don't know myself! Nobody would EVER recognise me!'

'Perfect!' said Dick, at once. 'You've hit the nail right on the head. Nobody *would* recognise you now. Your dad was right to say cut your hair off and dress up as a boy. Any prowling kidnapper would never think *you* were Berta, the pretty little girl.'

'I'd rather be kidnapped than look like this,' wept Berta. 'What will the girls at your school say, Anne, when they see me?'

'They don't say anything to George about her short hair, and they won't say anything to you,' said Anne.

'Stop crying, Bert – er – Lesley,' said Aunt Fanny. 'You make me feel quite upset. You've been very good to sit so still all that time. I'll have to think of a little reward for you.'

Berta stopped crying at once.

'Please,' she said, 'there's only one thing I want now. I want Sally-dog to sleep with me.'

'Oh dear, Ber – er Lesley – I really *can't* have another dog in that little bedroom,' said poor Aunt Fanny. 'And George would make things very unpleasant if I did.'

'Aunt Fanny – Sally is a very very good guard for me,' said Berta. 'She barks at the very slightest sound. I'd feel safe with her in the bedroom.'

'I'd like you to have her,' said Aunt Fanny, 'but . . .'

Joanna had come into the room to put away some things and had heard the conversation. She stared in admiration at Berta's neat golden head, and then made a suggestion.

'Berta could have her camp bed in my room,' she said. 'I don't mind the dog a bit, she can have her and welcome, she's a pet, that little poodle. It's very crowded in the girls' room now, with three beds in it, and my room's a nice big one. So, if Berta doesn't mind sharing it, she's welcome.'

'Oh Joanna – that's good of you,' said Aunt Fanny, relieved at such a simple solution. 'Also, your room is up in the attic – it'd be very difficult for kidnappers to find their way there – and nobody would think of looking into your room for one of the children.'

'*Thank* you, Joanna, you're just *wunnerful*!' said Berta in delight. 'Sally, do you hear that? You'll be sleeping on my feet tonight, like Timmy does on George's.'

'I don't really approve of that, you know, Berta,' said Aunt Fanny. 'Oh dear – I called you Berta again. Lesley, I mean. What a muddle I'm going to get into! Dick, get the dustpan and sweep up the hair on the floor.'

When Julian and George came back there was no sign of the golden hair on the floor. They put their parcels down on the table and shouted for Aunt Fanny. 'Mum!' called George.

'Aunt Fanny!' shouted Julian.

She came running downstairs with Berta and Anne and Dick. Julian and George looked at Berta, thunderstruck.

'Is it *really* you, Berta?' said Julian. 'I didn't recognise you!'

'You *do* look like a boy!' said George. 'I never thought you would.'

'A good-looking boy,' said Julian. 'Your dad was right. It's the best disguise you could have!'

'Where are the clothes?' asked Berta, rather pleased at all the interest in her looks. They opened the parcels and pulled out the things.

They weren't really very exciting – a boy's raincoat in navy blue, two pairs of boy's jeans, two jumpers, a few T-shirts and a pair of swimming trunks.

'And shoes and socks,' said George. 'But we decided you'd got plenty of socks that would do, so we only bought one pair of those. Oh – and here's a boy's cap! We bought it just for fun.'

Berta put on the cap at once. There were squeals of laughter from everyone. 'It suits her! She's got it on at just the right angle. She looks a real boy!'

'*You* put it on, George,' said Berta, and George took it, eager to share in the admiration. But it looked ridiculous on her curls, and wouldn't sit down flat as it should. Everyone hooted.

'It makes you look a girl! Take it off!'

George took it off in disappointment. How very aggravating that this girl Berta should make a better boy than she did! She threw the cap on the table, half cross that they had bought it.

'Go upstairs and put some of the things on,' said Aunt Fanny, amused at all these goings-on.

Up went Berta obediently, and soon came down again, wearing jeans and a T-shirt. Everyone roared with laughter. Berta was now quite enjoying herself and paraded around the room, her cap tilted on one side of her head.

'She looks like a very tidy, neat little boy, a good and angelic child!' said Julian. 'Lesley, you'll have to get yourself a bit dirty – you look too good to be true.'

'I don't like getting dirty,' said Berta. 'I think—'

But what she thought nobody knew because at that moment the door opened and Uncle Quentin came into the room.

'I'd like to know how you think I can do my work with all this hooting and cackling going on,' he began, and then he suddenly saw Berta, and stopped.

'Who's this?' he said, looking Berta up and down.

'Don't you know, Dad?' said George.

'Of course not. Never seen him in my life before!' said her father. 'Don't tell me it's somebody else come to stay.'

'It's Berta,' said Anne, with a giggle.

'Berta – now who's Berta?' said Uncle Quentin, frowning. 'I seem to have heard that name before.'

'The girl you thought might be kidnapped,' explained Dick.

'Oh *Berta* – Elbur's girl!' said Uncle Quentin. 'I remember *her* all right. But who's *this*? This boy? I've never seen *him* before. What's your name, boy?'

'Lesley,' said Berta. 'But I was Berta when you saw me at breakfast.'

'Good heavens!' said Uncle Quentin, amazed. 'What a – what a transformation! Your own dad wouldn't know you. I hope I remember who you are. Keep reminding me, if I don't.'

Off he went, back to his study. The children laughed, and Aunt Fanny had to laugh too.

'By the way,' she said, 'I want you all to have lunch at home today, because it's really too late now to start making sandwiches for a picnic; it's only cold ham and salad, so don't get *too* hungry, will you?'

'Is there time for a swim?' asked Julian, looking at his watch.

'Yes – if you'll come in about twelve o'clock and pick the fruit for a pudding for lunch,' said his aunt. 'It takes ages to pick enough for eight people, and Joanna and I have a lot to do today.'

'Right. We'll go for a swim now, and then we'll ALL pick fruit,' said Julian. 'Bagsie I pick the plums. The raspberries are such fiddly little things.'

'I'll wear a long T-shirt over the swimming trunks, so that'll be all right,' said Berta. 'Boys often do that.'

Berta's cases were now all in Joanna's big room and she ran to get changed.

'Bring a towel,' yelled George, and went into her own room with Anne.

'I bet Berta can't swim,' she said. 'That'll be a pity. We'll have to teach her.'

'Well, don't duck her too often!' said Anne, seeing a look in George's eye that wasn't too kindly. 'Oh no – my swimming costume isn't here – I'm sure I brought it in from the clothes line.'

It took quite a while to find it, and the boys and Berta had already gone down to the beach with Sally by the time Anne and George were ready to follow with the impatient Timmy.

They were down on the beach at last, and there was Sally-dog guarding the things belonging to Julian, Dick and Berta. She was lying on them, and she even dared to growl at Timmy when he came near.

George laughed. 'Growl back, Timmy! Don't let a little snippet like that give you cheek. Growl back!'

But Timmy wouldn't. He just sat down out of reach of Sally, and looked at her sadly. Wasn't she friends with him any more?

'Where are the others?' said Anne, shading her eyes from the glare of the sun and looking out to sea. 'Look how far out they've swum! That *can't* be Berta with them, surely!'

George looked out over the stretch of blue sea at once. She saw three heads bobbing. Yes, Berta *was* out there!

'She must be a really good swimmer,' said Anne, admiringly. 'I couldn't swim out as far as that. We were wrong about Berta. She swims like a fish!'

George said nothing. She ran to the waves, plunged through a big one just as it was curling over, and swam out strongly. She couldn't *believe* that it was Berta out there! And if it was, the boys must be helping her!

But it *was* Berta. Her golden head glistened wet in the water, and she shouted in glee as she swam.

'This is great! This is wunnerful! Gee, I'm enjoying this! Hi George – isn't the water warm?'

Julian and Dick grinned at the panting George.

'Lesley's a great swimmer,' said Dick. 'She nearly beat me once. She'd beat *you*, George!'

'She wouldn't,' said George, but all the same she didn't challenge Berta to a race!

It was fun to be five, fun to chase one another in the sea, to swim under the water and grab somebody's leg. And Anne laughed till she choked when she saw somebody heave themselves out of the water right on to George's back, and duck her well and truly.

It was Berta! And what was more, the angry George couldn't catch her afterwards. Berta could swim much too fast!

## 9  *A sudden phone call*

Berta soon settled down happily with the Five. George couldn't bear to think that the girl had to be dressed like a boy, but her jealousy wore off a little as the days went by – although she couldn't help feeling annoyed that Berta was such a good swimmer!

She could dive well too, and swim under water even longer than the boys could, much to their surprise.

'Oh well, you see, back home, we've got a pool in our garden,' she said. 'A wonDERful pool, gee, you should see it. And I learnt to swim in it when I was two. Pops always called me a water-baby.'

Berta ate just as much as the others, although she wasn't as sturdy and well built. She was loud in her praise of the meals, and this pleased Aunt Fanny and Joanna very much.

'You're getting fatter, Lesley,' said Aunt Fanny a week later, looking at her as she sat eating her lunch with the others. 'And what's better still – you're getting out in the open air. You're almost as tanned as the others!'

'Yes. I thought so too,' said Berta, pleased.

'It's a good thing you caught the sun so easily,' said Aunt Fanny. 'Now, if any kidnappers come around looking for a long-haired pale-faced American girl, they'd take one look at the lot of you and off they'd go! Nobody would guess you were Berta!'

'All the same, I'd much rather *be* Berta,' said Berta. 'I still don't like pretending to be a boy. It's silly, and it makes me *feel* silly. Anyway, thank goodness my hair's growing a bit longer. I don't look *quite* so much like a boy now!'

'You're right,' said Aunt Fanny, and everyone looked at Berta. 'I'll have to cut it short again.'

'Oh no!' said Berta. 'Why did I say that? You wouldn't have noticed if I hadn't mentioned it. Let it grow again, please, Aunt Fanny. I've been here a week and there isn't even a *smell* of a kidnapper – and I reckon there won't be either!'

But Aunt Fanny was firm about the hair, and after the meal she made Berta sit still while she clipped it a little shorter. It wasn't curly like

George's, and now that it was short, the wave had almost gone from it. She really did look like a good clean little boy!

'A wishy-washy one!' said George, unkindly, but everyone knew what she meant.

Sally the poodle was a great success. Even George couldn't go on disliking the happy, dancing little dog. She trotted and capered about on her slim little legs, and Timmy was her adoring slave.

'She always looks as if she's running about on tiptoe,' said Anne, and so she did. She made friends with everyone, even the paper-boy, who was really scared of dogs.

Uncle Quentin was the only one who didn't get used to Berta and Sally. When he met them together, Berta so like a small boy, Sally at her heels, he stopped and stared.

'Now let me see – who are you?' he said. 'Yes – you're Berta!'

'No – he's LESLEY!' everyone would say.

'You *mustn't* call her Berta, dear,' said his wife. 'You really mustn't. It's a funny thing that you never could remember she was Berta, and now that we've made her into Lesley, you immediately remember she's Berta!'

'You've made her look exactly like a boy,' said Uncle Quentin, much to George's annoyance. George was beginning to be afraid that Berta looked more boyish than she did! 'Well, I hope you're having a good time with the others, er – er . . .'

'*Lesley* is the name,' said Aunt Fanny with a little laugh. 'Quentin, please try and remember.'

Another day passed peacefully by, and the five children and two dogs were out of doors all day long, swimming, boating, exploring, really enjoying themselves.

Berta wanted to go over to Kirrin Island, but George kept making excuses not to go.

'Don't be mean,' said Dick. 'We *all* want to go. It's ages since we went. It's just that you don't want to let Lesley do something she'd like to do!'

'It isn't,' said George. 'Perhaps we'll go tomorrow.'

But when tomorrow came something happened that upset their plans for going to Kirrin Island. A phone call came for Uncle Quentin, and immediately he was in a panic.

'Fanny! Fanny, where are you?' he called. 'I have to leave straight away. Straight away, do you hear?'

His wife came running down the stairs at top speed. 'Quentin, why? What's happened?'

'Elbur's found a mistake in our calculations,' said Uncle Quentin. 'What nonsense! There's no mistake. None at all.'

'But why can't he come *here* and work it out with you?' asked his wife. 'Why have *you* got to rush off like this? Tell him to come here, Quentin. I'll find him a bed somehow.'

'He says he doesn't want to, while his daughter – his daughter – what's her name now?'

'*Lesley*,' said his wife. 'All right, don't bother to explain. I see now that it'd be foolish for him to come while Lesley's here – she'd be calling him Pops, and—'

'Pops?' said her husband, startled. 'What do you mean – Pops?'

'It's what she calls her dad,' said Aunt Fanny, patiently. 'Anyway, he's right. It'd be foolish to hide Lesley here so well, and then have everyone hear her calling him Pops, and him calling her Berta – if any kidnappers followed him,

they'd soon find out where his daughter was –
here, with our four!'

'Yes – that's what I was trying to tell you,'
said her husband, impatiently. 'Anyway I have
go to Elbur straight away. I'll be back in two
days' time.'

'In that case I'll go with you, Quentin,' said his
wife. 'I could do with a quiet two days – and
you're not much good when you're alone, are you
– losing your socks, and forgetting to have your
meals, and . . .'

Her husband gave a sudden smile that lit up his
face and made him seem quite young. 'Will you
really come with me? I thought you'd hate to
leave the children.'

'It's only for two days,' said his wife. 'And
Joanna's very good with them. I'll arrange that
they'll go out on all-day picnics in the boat –
they'll be safe then. If any kidnappers *were* around
they'd find it difficult to snatch Lesley out of a
boat! But I'm beginning not to believe that tale of
Elbur's. He just got into a panic when he heard
the rumour, I expect.'

The children were told of the sudden decision
when they got back to lunch that day. Joanna had

to tell them, because Aunt Fanny and her husband had already left, complete with two suitcases, one containing precious papers and the other clothes for two days.

'Oh!' said Julian, surprised. 'I hope nothing horrible's happened.'

'Oh no – it was just a sudden phone call from Lesley's dad,' said Joanna, smiling at Berta. 'He had to see your uncle in a hurry – about some figures.'

'Why didn't Pops come down here – then he could have seen *me*?' demanded Berta at once.

'Because everyone would have known who you are, then,' said Dick. 'We're *hiding* you, don't forget!'

'I think I *had* forgotten,' said Berta, rather surprised at herself. 'It's so *lovely* down here in Kirrin with you all. The days seem to *swim* by!'

'Your mum said you'd better go off on all-day picnics in the boat,' said Joanna to George. 'That was to make things easy for me, of course. But I don't mind what you do – you can come back to lunch each day, if you like.'

'I do like you, Joanna!' said Berta, giving

the surprised cook a sudden hug. 'You're a real honey!'

'In fact, she's wunnerful!' said Dick. 'It's all right, Joanna – we'll go out for lunch, *and* for tea, till my aunt comes back. And we'll make the sandwiches and pack up everything ourselves.'

'Well, that's nice of you,' said Joanna. 'Why don't you go across to Kirrin Island for the day? Lesley keeps wanting to go.'

Berta grinned at Joanna.

'We'll go if the boat's ready,' said George, rather reluctantly. 'You know Alf's mending one of the rowlocks. Let's go and see if it's finished.'

They all went to see, but Alf wasn't there. His father was working on another boat, over by the jetty, and he called to them.

'Do you want my Alf? He's gone off in his uncle's boat for a day's fishing. He said to tell you the rowlock's not mended yet, but he'll do it tonight when he comes back.'

'Right. Thank you,' called back Julian. Berta looked very disappointed. 'Cheer up,' he said. 'We'll be able to go tomorrow.'

'We won't,' said Berta, mournfully. 'Something else will happen to stop us – or George'll think of another excuse not to go. Gee, if I had a wunnerful – wonDERful – island like that, I'd go and *live* on it.'

They went back to Kirrin Cottage and packed up a very good lunch for themselves. Berta's father had sent down a parcel of American goodies three days before, and they wanted to try them.

'Snick-snacks!' said Dick, reading the name on a tin. 'Shrimp, lobster, crab and a dozen other things all in one tin. Sounds good. We'll make sandwiches with this!'

'Gorgies,' said Anne, reading the name on another tin. 'What a strange name! Oh – I suppose it's something you *gorge* yourself with. Let's open it.'

They opened half a dozen tins with very exciting names and made themselves so many sandwiches that Joanna exclaimed in amazement. 'How many have you made for each of you?'

'Twenny each – I mean twenTY,' said Berta. 'But we won't be back to lunch or tea, Joanna. I guess we'll be plenny hungry.'

'PlenTY!' chorused everyone, and Berta obediently repeated the word, a grin on her suntanned face.

What a day they had! They walked for miles and picnicked in a shady wood near a little stream that bubbled along nearby, sounding very cool and enticing. They decided to sit with their feet in it as they ate, and Anne gave continual little squeals because she said the water tickled the soles of her feet.

They were so tired when they got home that night that it was all they could do to eat their supper and stagger upstairs to bed.

'I won't wake till half past eleven tomorrow morning,' yawned Dick. 'Oh my poor feet! I'm so tired I'll probably fall asleep cleaning my teeth.'

'What a peaceful night!' said Anne, looking out of her window. 'Well – sleep tight, everyone. I don't expect any of us will open an eye till late tomorrow morning. I know I won't!'

But she did. She opened both eyes very wide indeed in the middle of the night.

## 10 *A puzzling thing*

All was quiet at Kirrin Cottage. The two boys slept soundly in their room, and George and Anne slept without stirring in theirs. Berta was up in Joanna's attic room, and hadn't moved since she had flopped into bed.

Timmy was on George's feet, as usual, and Sally the poodle was curled up in the crook of Berta's knees, looking like a ball of black wool! Nobody stirred.

A black cloud crept up the sky and blotted out the stars one by one. Then a low roll of thunder came. It was far off, and only a rumble, but it woke both the dogs, and it woke Anne too.

She opened her eyes, wondering what the noise was. Then she knew – it was thunder.

'Oh, I hope a storm won't come and break up this wonderful weather!' she thought, as she lay and listened. She turned towards the open window and looked for the stars, but there were none to see.

'If a storm's coming, I'll go and watch it at the window,' thought Anne. 'It should be a magnificent sight over Kirrin Bay. I'm so hot too – I'd like a breath of fresh air at the window!'

She got quietly out of bed and padded over to the open window. She leaned out, sniffing the cool air outside. The night was very dark indeed, because of the great black cloud.

The thunder came again, but not very near – just a low growl. Timmy jumped off George's bed and went to join Anne. He put his great paws up on the windowsill and looked out solemnly over the bay.

And then both he and Anne heard another sound – a faraway chug-chug-chug-chug-chug.

'It's a motorboat,' said Anne, listening. 'Isn't it Timmy? Someone's having a very late trip! Can you see any ship lights, Tim? I can't.'

The engine of the motorboat cut out just then, and there was complete silence except for the swish-swash-swish of the waves on the beach. Anne strained her eyes to see if she could spot any light anywhere to show where the motorboat was. It sounded quite far out in the bay. Why had it stopped on the water? Why hadn't it gone to the jetty?

Then she did see a light, but a very faint one, right out at the entrance of the bay, about the middle. It shone for a while, moved here and there, and then disappeared. Anne was puzzled.

'Surely that's just about where Kirrin Island is?' she whispered to Timmy. 'Is anyone there? Has the motorboat gone there, do you think? Let's listen to see if it leaves again and goes away.'

But no further sound came from across the bay, and no light shone either. 'Perhaps the motorboat's *behind* Kirrin Island,' thought Anne, suddenly. 'And then I wouldn't be able to see any lights on it – the island would hide the boat *and* its lights. But what was that *moving* light I saw? *Was* it someone on the island? My eyes are getting so sleepy again that I can hardly keep them open. Perhaps I didn't hear or see anything after all!'

There was no more thunder, and no lightning at all. The big black cloud began to thin out and one or two stars appeared in the gaps. Anne yawned and crawled into bed. Timmy jumped back on George's bed and curled himself up with a little sigh.

In the morning Anne had almost forgotten her watch at the open window the night before. It was only when Joanna mentioned that a big storm had burst over a town fifty miles away that Anne remembered the thunder she'd heard.

'Oh!' she said, suddenly. 'Yes – *I* heard thunder too, and I got out of bed, hoping to watch a storm. But it didn't come. And I heard a motorboat far out in the bay, but I couldn't see any lights – except for a faint, moving one I thought was on Kirrin Island.'

George sat up in her chair as if she'd had an electric shock. 'On Kirrin Island! What do you mean? Nobody's there. *Nobody's* allowed there!'

'Well – I may have been wrong,' said Anne. 'I was so sleepy. I didn't hear the motorboat go away. I just went back to bed.'

'You *could* have woken me, if you thought you saw a light on my island,' said George. 'You really should have!'

'Oh, Anne – it wouldn't be kidnappers, would it?' said Joanna, at once.

Julian laughed. 'No, Joanna. What would be the use of them going to Kirrin Island? They couldn't do any kidnapping there, in full view of all the houses around the bay!'

'I guess it was only a dream, Anne,' said Berta. 'I guess you heard the thunder in your sleep, and it turned into the sound of a motorboat chugging – dreams *do* that sort of thing. Once I left the tap running in my basin when I went to sleep, and I dreamed all night long I was riding over Niagara Falls!'

Everyone laughed. Berta could be very funny at times.

'If the boat's ready, we'll definitely go over to Kirrin Island today,' said George. 'If any tourists are there I'll send Timmy after them!'

'There'll only be the rabbits,' said Dick. 'I wonder if there are still hundreds there – last time we went they were so tame that we nearly fell over them!'

'Yes – but we didn't have Timmy with us,' said Anne. 'George, it *will* be nice to go to Kirrin Island again. We'll have to tell Lesley about the adventures we've had there.'

They washed up after breakfast, made the beds and did their rooms. Joanna put her head around Julian's bedroom door.

'Will you want a packed lunch for a picnic

again, Julian?' she said. 'If you don't, I can get you a nice bit of cold ham for lunch. The grocer's just rung up.'

'If the boat's mended, we're going over to the island, Joanna,' said Julian. 'And then we'd like a packed lunch. But if we don't go, we'll stay for lunch. It'll be easier for you in a way, won't it? We all got up so late this morning that there's not much time to make sandwiches and pick fruit and so on.'

'Well, you tell me, as soon as you know about the boat,' said Joanna, and disappeared.

George came in.

'I'm going to see if the boat's mended,' she said. 'I'll only be gone a minute. Joanna wants to know.'

She was back almost at once.

'It's not ready,' she said, disappointed. 'But it'll be ready at two o'clock this afternoon. So we'll have lunch here, shall we, and then go over to the island afterwards? We'll pack up a picnic tea.'

'Right,' said Julian. 'Let's swim at the beach this morning, then. The tide will be nice and high and we can have some fun with the big breakers.'

'And also keep an eye on Alf to see that he keeps his word about the boat,' said Dick.

So, when all their jobs were finished – and they were very conscientious about them – the five children and the two dogs went off down to the beach. It was a little cooler after the thunder, but not much, and they were warm enough in their swimming things, with jackets to wear after a swim.

'There's nothing nicer than to feel hot and go into the sea and get cool, and then come out and get hot in the sun again, and then go back into the sea,' began Berta.

'You say that every single day!' said George. 'It's like a record! Still, I agree with you! Come on – let's have a good swim!'

They all plunged through the big, curling breakers, squealing as the water dashed over their bodies, cold and stinging. They chased one another, swam under water and grabbed at the legs swimming there, floated on their backs, and wished they hadn't forgotten to bring the big red beach ball with them. But nobody wanted to go and fetch it so they had to do without it.

Timmy and Sally raced about in the shallow

waves at the edge of the sea. Timmy was a good swimmer, but Sally didn't much like the water, so they always played together at the edge. They were very funny to watch.

The dogs were glad when the children came panting out of the water. They lay down on the warm beach and Timmy flopped down beside George. She pushed him away.

'You smell of seaweed,' she said. 'Ugh!'

After a while Dick sat up to pull on his jacket. He gazed over the bay to where Kirrin Island lay basking in the sun and gave a sudden exclamation.

'Look, all of you!'

Everyone sat up.

'There's someone on Kirrin Island, although I can't see them,' said Dick. 'Someone lying down, looking through binoculars at our beach. Can you see the sun glittering on the lenses?'

'Yes!' said Julian. 'You're right! Someone must be using binoculars to examine this beach. We can't see them as you say – but it's easy enough to see the sunlight glinting on the lenses. What a cheek!'

'Cheek!' said George, her face crimson with

rage. 'It's a lot more than cheek! How *dare* people go on my island and use it to spy on people on the beach? Let's spy on *them*! Let's get our own binoculars and look through them. We'll see who it is, then!'

'I'll get them,' said Dick and ran off to Kirrin Cottage.

He felt worried. It seemed a strange thing to do – to spy on people sitting on the beach around the bay, using binoculars on Kirrin Island. What was the reason?

He came back with the binoculars, and handed them to Julian.

'I think they're gone now, whoever it was,' said Julian. 'I don't mean gone off the island, but gone somewhere else on it. We can't see the glint of the sun on their binoculars any more.'

'Well, hurry up and see if you can spot anyone through *our* binoculars,' said George, impatiently.

Julian adjusted them, and gazed through them earnestly. The island seemed very near indeed when seen through the powerful binoculars. Everyone watched him anxiously.

'See anyone?' asked Dick.

'Not a soul,' said Julian, disappointed.

He handed the binoculars to the impatient George, who put them to her eyes at once.

'That's so annoying!' she said. 'There's not a thing to be seen, not a thing. Whoever it was has gone into hiding somewhere. If it's tourists having a picnic there I'll be absolutely furious. If we see smoke rising we'll know it is tourists!'

But no smoke arose. Dick had a turn at looking through the binoculars, and he looked puzzled. He took them down from his eyes and turned to the others.

'We ought to be able to see the rabbits running about,' he said. 'But I can't see a single one. Did either of you, Julian and George?'

'Well – now I come to think of it – no, I didn't,' said Julian, and George said the same.

'They were frightened by whoever was there, of course,' said Dick. 'Do you think it'll be all right to take Lesley with us when we go to the island this afternoon? I mean – it's just a bit *odd* that anyone should be using the island to spy from.'

'Yes. I see what you mean,' said Julian. 'If it occurred to the kidnappers, whoever they are, that Berta might be down here with us, it'd be a good idea to land on the island and spy on the beach from there. They'd guess we'd come down to swim every day.'

'Yes. And they'd see five children instead of four and would start to ask questions about the fifth!' said Dick. 'They'd hope actually to see Berta on the beach – they've probably got a photograph of her – and they'd be looking for a girl with long wavy hair.'

'And there isn't one!' said Anne. 'Mine's not wavy and it's not right down to my shoulders as Lesley's was. They'd be confused!'

'There's one thing that'd tell them that Berta was here though,' said Julian, suddenly.

He pointed to Sally.

'Oh yes!' said Dick. 'Sally would give the game away all right! We'll have to think about all this!'

## 11 On Kirrin Island again

George wanted to get her boat and go across to the island immediately. She was so furious at the thought of anyone else being there without permission that all she wanted to do was to chase them away.

But Julian said no.

'For one thing the boat won't be ready till two,' he said. 'For another thing we've got to think about whether it's a sensible thing to do, to go to the island *if* possible kidnappers are here, on the lookout for Berta – Lesley, I mean.'

'We could go without her,' said George. 'We could leave her safely with Joanna.'

'That'd be a silly thing to do,' said Dick. 'Anyone watching us coming across in the boat would see that one of the five was missing, and would guess at once it was Berta. If we go, *all* of us should go.'

'Actually I think it might be a good thing to

do,' said Julian. 'Carry the war right into the enemy's camp, so to speak – if there *are* enemies! It'd be really useful if we could see what they're like and give a description to the police. I vote we go.'

'*Yes*!' said Dick. 'Anyway, we'll have Tim with us. He can deal with any bad behaviour from the intruders!'

'I don't really think it's anybody but tourists,' said Julian. 'I think we're making too much of the whole thing just because someone gazed at the beach through binoculars!'

'Remember that I think I saw a light on the island last night,' Anne reminded him.

'Yes, I'd forgotten that,' said Julian, looking at his watch. 'It's almost lunch-time. Let's go and have something to eat, and then fetch the boat. Alf's working on it now. We'll give him a shout to see if it'll be ready at two.'

Alf was called, and he shouted back. 'Yes! Be ready sharp at two o'clock, if you want her. I've done one or two little jobs on her besides the rowlock.'

'That's good,' said Dick, and they walked back to Kirrin Cottage. 'We'll soon find out who's on your island, George – and if they refuse to leave, we'll have a bit of fun with Timmy! He can round them up all right, can't you, Tim!'

'So could Sally,' said Berta. 'Sally's teeth aren't very big, but they're sharp. She once went for a man who accidentally pushed into me, and you should have seen the nips she gave him, all down his leg!'

'Yes. Sally would come in useful,' said Dick.

George looked rather scornful. That silly little poodle! she thought. A fat lot of good *she'd* be! Timmy's worth a hundred of her!

Joanna had a wonderful lunch ready for them – ham and salad and new potatoes piled high in a big dish. There were firm red tomatoes from the greenhouse, and lettuces with enormous yellow-green hearts, crisp radishes, and a whole cucumber ready for anyone to cut as they liked. Slices of hard-boiled egg were mixed in with the salad, and Joanna had put in tiny boiled carrots and peas as well.

'What a salad!' said Dick. 'Fit for a king!'

'And big enough for *several* kings!' said Anne. 'How many potatoes, Ju? Small or large ones?'

Julian looked at the piled-up dish.

'I love these potatoes!' he said. 'I'll have three large and four small.'

'What's for pudding?' asked Berta. 'I like this kind of salad so much that I might not have room for a stodgy sort of pudding.'

'It's fresh raspberries from the garden, sugar and home-made ice-cream,' said Joanna. 'I didn't think you'd want a hot pudding. My sister came to see me this morning, so I got her to pick the raspberries for me.'

'I can't think of a nicer meal than this,' said Berta, helping herself to the salad. 'I really can't. I like your meals better than the ones we have at home in America.'

'We'll turn you into a proper little English boy before you know where you are!' said Dick.

They told Joanna about what they'd seen that morning on the island. She took a serious view of it at once.

'Now you know what your aunt said, Julian,' she said. 'The police have got to have a report of anything suspicious. You'd better ring them up.'

'I will when we've been over to the island and back,' said Julian. 'I don't want to look like an idiot, Joanna. If it's only harmless tourists who don't know any better there's no need to bother the police. I *promise* to ring the police if we find anything suspicious.'

'I think you ought to ring them *now*,' said Joanna. 'And I don't think you ought to go over to the island if you're suspicious of the people there.'

'We'll have Timmy with us,' said Dick. 'Don't worry.'

'And Sally too,' added Berta at once.

Joanna said no more, but went out to get the raspberries and ice-cream, looking worried. She brought in an enormous glass dish of fresh red raspberries and another dish of creamy-looking ice-cream blocks from the fridge.

A sigh of admiration went up from everyone.

'Who could want anything better?' said Dick. 'And that ice-cream – how do you get it like that, Joanna – not too frozen and not too melty? Just how I like it. I hope some American doesn't get hold of you and whisk you away across the ocean – you're worth your weight in gold!'

Joanna laughed. 'You say such extravagant things, Dick – and all because of an ordinary dish like raspberries and ice-cream. Lesley will tell you there's nothing clever about raspberries and ice-cream.'

'I agree with every word the others say,' said Berta fervently. 'You're wunnerful, you're a honey, you're . . .'

But Joanna had run out of the room, laughing, very pleased. She didn't mind what she did for children like these!

After they'd finished lunch, they went down to the beach. Alf was still with the boat.

'She's finished!' he called. 'You going out in her now? I'll give you a hand down with her, then.'

Soon all five children and the dogs as well were in George's boat. The boys took the oars and began to pull hard towards the island. Timmy stood at the prow as he loved to do, forepaws on the edge of the boat, looking out across the water.

'He fancies himself as a figurehead,' said Dick. 'Look, here comes Sally – she wants to be one too. Mind you don't fall overboard, Sally, and get your pretty feet wet. You'll have to learn to swim if you do!'

Sally stood close beside Timmy, and both dogs looked eagerly towards the island – Timmy because he knew there were hundreds of rabbits there, and Sally because for her it was still quite an adventure to go out in a boat like this.

Berta, too, gazed eagerly at the little island as they drew near. She had heard so many tales about it now! She looked especially at the old castle rising up from it. It was in ruins, and Berta thought it must be very old indeed. Like many Americans, she loved old buildings and old customs. How lucky George was to own an island like this!

Rocks guarded the island, and the sea ran strongly over them, sending up spray and foam.

'How are we going to get safely to the shore?' said Berta, rather alarmed at the array of fierce-looking rocks that guarded the island.

'There's a little cove we always use,' said George.

She was at the tiller, and she steered the boat cleverly in and out of the rocks. They rounded a low wall of very sharp rocks and Berta suddenly saw the little cove.

'Oh – is that the cove you mean?' she said. 'It's like a little harbour going right up to that stretch of sand!'

There was a smooth inlet of water running

between rocks, making a natural little harbour, as Berta said. The boat slid smoothly into the inlet and up to the beach of sand.

Dick leapt out and pulled it up the shore.

'She's safe here,' he told Berta. 'Welcome to Kirrin Island!'

Berta laughed. She felt very happy. What a wonderful place to come to!

George led the way up the sandy beach to the rocks behind, and they climbed over them. They stopped at the top, and Berta exclaimed in amazement.

'Rabbits! Thousands of them! Absolutely thousands. I never saw such tame ones in my life. Will they let me pick them up?'

'No,' said George. 'They're not as tame as that! They'll run away when we go near – but they probably won't go into their holes. They know us – we've so often been here.'

Sally the poodle was amazed at the rabbits. She couldn't believe her eyes. She stood close beside Berta, staring at the scuttling rabbits, her nose twitching as she tried to get their smell. She couldn't understand why Timmy didn't run at them.

Timmy stood still beside George, his tail down, looking very depressed. A visit to Kirrin Island wasn't as much fun for him as it was for the children, because he wasn't allowed to hunt the rabbits. *What* a waste of rabbits!

'Poor Tim! Look at him!' said Julian. 'He looks so miserable. Look at Sally, too – she's longing to go after the rabbits, but she doesn't think it's good manners to chase them till Timmy does!'

Good manners or not, little Sally could bear it no longer! She suddenly made a dart at a rabbit who had come temptingly near, and it leapt into the air in fright.

'Sally!' called George, in a very sharp tone. 'NO! You're not to chase my rabbits! Tim – go and fetch her here!'

Timmy went off to Sally and gave a tiny little growl. Sally looked at him in amazement. Could her friend Timmy *really* be growling at her? Timmy began to push himself against her and she found herself being shepherded over to George.

'Good dog, Timmy,' said George, pleased to have shown everyone how obedient he was. 'Sally, you mustn't chase these rabbits, because they're too tame! They haven't learnt to run away properly yet, because not many people come here and frighten them.'

'Whoever was here this morning scared them all right,' said Julian, remembering. 'Don't let's forget there may be people here. Well – I can't see anyone so far!'

They went cautiously forward, towards the old castle, Timmy running ahead. Then Julian stopped and pointed to the ground.

'Cigarette ends – look! Fresh ones, too. There are definitely people here. Walk ahead of us, Tim.'

But at that moment there came the sound that Anne had heard the night before – the sound of a motorboat's engine. R-r-r-r-r-r-r!

'They're escaping!' cried Dick. 'Quick, run to the other side of the island! We might see them!'

## 12  Very suspicious

The children, with the two dogs barking excitedly, ran to the other, seaward side of the island. Great rocks lay out there, and the sea splashed over them.

'There it is – a motorboat!' cried Dick.

They all stood and watched the boat riding over the sea at a very fast speed.

'Where are the binoculars – did we bring them with us?' said Julian. 'I'd like to focus them on the boat and see if I can read the name – or even see the men in it!'

But the binoculars had been left behind at Kirrin Cottage – what a pity!

'They must have anchored their motorboat out there, and somehow clambered inshore over the rocks,' said George. 'It's a dangerous thing to do if you don't know the best way.'

'Yes – and if they came last night, as I think they must have done, because I'm sure now it was the engine of the motorboat that I heard,' said Anne, 'if they came last night, they must have clambered to the shore in the dark. I wonder how they managed it!'

'It must have been the light of a torch you saw on the island in the night,' said Julian. 'They probably didn't want to be seen arriving on the island, and that's why they went to the other side, the seaward side. I wonder if they were spying to find out if Berta is with us or not.'

'Let's snoop around a bit more and see if we can find anything else,' said Anne. 'The motorboat's almost out of sight now.'

They went back to the other side of the island. Berta looked with awe at the old castle in the middle. Jackdaws circled around a tower, calling loudly. 'Chack-chack-chack!'

'Once my castle had strong walls all around it,' said George. 'And there were two great towers. One's almost in ruins, as you can see, but the other's fairly good. Come right into the castle.'

Berta followed the others in, silent with awe. To think that this island, and this wonderful old ruined castle, belonged to George! How very, very lucky she was!

She went through a great doorway, and found herself in a dark room, with stone walls enclosing it. Two narrow, slit-like windows brought in all the light there was.

'It's strange and old and mysterious,' said Berta, half to herself. 'It's asleep and dreaming of the old days when people lived here. It doesn't like us being here!'

'Wake up!' said Dick. 'You look all daydreamy!'

Berta shook herself and looked around again. Then she went on through the castle and looked at other rooms, some without roofs, some without one or two of their walls.

'It's a honey of a castle!' she said to George. 'A real honey. Wunnerful. WonDERful.'

They wandered all around, showing the awestruck Berta everything.

'We'll show you the dungeons too,' said George, very pleased to be impressing Berta so much.

'Dungeons! You've got dungeons too – oh, of course, you told me about them,' said Berta. '*Dungeons*! I'll never forget this afternoon.'

As they walked over the old courtyard Timmy suddenly growled and stood still, his tail down, the hackles on his neck rising. Everyone automatically stood still too.

'What is it, Tim?' asked George, in a whisper.

Timmy's nose was pointing towards the little harbour where they'd left their boat.

'There must be someone there,' said Dick. 'Don't say they're going off with our boat!'

George gave a scream. Her boat! Her precious boat! She set off at top speed with Timmy bounding in front.

'Come back, George – there may be danger!' shouted Julian, but George didn't listen.

She ran over the rocks that led down to the little harbour beach, and then stopped still in surprise.

Two policemen were walking up the sandy beach! Their boat was drawn up beside George's. They saluted her and grinned.

'Afternoon, George!'

'What are you doing on my island?' demanded George, recognising them. 'Why have you come here?'

'Someone reported suspicious people on the island,' said the first policeman.

'*Who* did?' said George. 'Nobody knew about

it but us!'

'I bet I know who reported it,' said Dick suddenly. 'Joanna did! She didn't like us going off by ourselves; she said we ought to phone the police.'

'That's right,' said the policeman. 'So we came to see for ourselves. Found anyone?'

Julian related how they'd first seen the cigarette ends, and then heard the motorboat starting up, and had gone to see it roaring away from the island.

'Ah,' said the policeman, profoundly. 'Ah!'

'What do you mean – "AH"?' asked Dick.

'Fred here heard a motorboat somewhere in the bay in the night,' said the first man. 'What was it doing there, I'd like to know?'

'So would we,' said Julian. '*We* saw someone on the island looking through binoculars at the beach this morning.'

This brought forth two more 'Ah's, and the policemen exchanged glances.

'Good thing you've got a couple of dogs with you,' said the one called Fred. 'Well – we'll just have a bit of a look around, and then we'll go back on our beats again. And make sure you ring us up next time anything turns up, OK?'

Off they went together, looking closely at the ground. They found the cigarette ends and picked them up. Then on they went again.

'Let's go back,' said George, in a low voice. 'It spoils things if other people are on the island. I don't want to have a picnic here now. Let's go off in the boat somewhere and have a picnic tea in a cove.'

So they dragged the boat down to the water and jumped in. Sally was very pleased to be back in the boat and ran from end to end wagging her stiff tail in delight. Timmy followed her up and down and got in everyone's way.

'How can I row if you keep on jumping over me, Timmy?' complained Dick. 'Sally, you're just as bad. Berta, are you all right? You look a bit green.'

'It's only excitement and the bumpy bit past the rocks,' said Berta, not wanting to appear seasick in front of the others. 'I'll be all right as soon as we get on to calm waters.'

But she wasn't, so it was regretfully decided that they must row to the shore. They had a lazy tea on the beach, and Berta recovered enough to join in heartily.

'Anyone got room for an ice-cream?' asked Anne. 'Because if so I'll go down to the shops and get some. I want to buy a new pair of shoelaces too. One of mine broke this morning.'

Everyone seemed to have room for an ice-cream, so Anne set off with Sally, who wanted to come with her. She went and got the laces, and then went to the café that sold ice-creams.

'Seven, please,' she said.

The girl in the shop smiled.

'Seven! You used to ask for five.'

'Yes, I know. But we've got someone staying with us – and another dog,' explained Anne. 'And both dogs like ice-creams.'

'That reminds me – someone was in here yesterday asking about your uncle,' said the girl. 'He said he knew him. He wanted to know how many children were staying at Kirrin Cottage, and I thought only the four of you were there – and Timmy, of course. He seemed surprised, and said, surely there was another girl?'

'Oh!' said Anne, startled. 'Did he really? How nosy! What did you say then?'

'I just said there were two boys and a girl, and

a girl who liked to dress as a boy,' said the girl.

Anne was glad that the girl hadn't known about Berta.

'What was the man like?' she asked.

'Just ordinary,' said the girl, trying to remember. 'He was wearing sunglasses. I noticed he had a large gold ring on his finger when he paid the bill. That's all I can remember.'

'Well, if anyone else asks you about us, just say we've got a friend staying with us called Lesley,' said Anne. 'Goodbye.'

She went off at top speed, anxious to tell the others. The man in the café must have been one of those who had gone to the island to watch the beach – he might have been staring at the five of them as they had played together. He must be one of the men now in the motorboat. Anne didn't like it, and it made her feel very worried.

She told the others what the girl had said as they sat in the sand and ate their ice-creams. Timmy gobbled his almost at once, and sat patiently watching Sally deal with hers, hoping that she'd leave some.

All the four listened intently to Anne's little story.

'That settles it,' said Dick. 'Those men are definitely snooping around trying to find out if Lesley's here.'

'They're getting too close,' said Julian.

'Still, your uncle and aunt come back tomorrow,' said Berta. 'We'll tell them, and maybe they'll have a good plan.'

'I hope those men don't know that they're away,' said Dick, uneasily. 'We'll have to keep a pretty close watch from now on. I wonder if Berta ought to stay on here with us.'

'See what Dad says tomorrow,' said George.

So it was decided that nothing should be done except to keep a sharp lookout until George's parents came back. They all went back to Kirrin Cottage and told Joanna what had happened on the island.

'You phoned the police, Joanna!' said Dick, shaking his finger at her.

'I did. And I was right to,' said Joanna. 'And what's more, Lesley's bed is going to be moved away from the window tonight *and* the window's going to be fastened even if we melt, *and* the door will be locked.'

'I'll lend you Timmy, too, if you like,' said

George. 'He can sleep in the room with Sally. You ought to be safe then!'

She really only meant it as a joke, but to her surprise Joanna accepted at once.

'Thank you,' she said. 'I'd be glad of Timmy. I feel all of a dither, left on my own like this, and kidnappers closing in on us!'

Julian laughed. 'It's not that bad, Joanna. Only one more night and Uncle Quentin and Aunt Fanny will be back.'

'Oh – I forgot to tell you,' said Joanna. 'A letter's arrived. They're staying away a whole week! That's why I feel so scared. A week – well, a lot can happen in a week!'

# 13  *A horrible shock*

Julian wasn't very happy to hear that his aunt and uncle were staying away for a week. He picked up the letter. It was addressed to George, but Joanna had opened it.

'Not returning for a week. Complications have arisen,' it said. 'Hope all's well. Love from Mum.'

There was no address. How annoying! Now Julian couldn't even let them *know* that he was feeling worried. He made up his mind to guard Berta every minute! Thank goodness they had Timmy. Nobody would dare to do any kidnapping under Timmy's eye!

He thought it was a good idea to put Timmy in Joanna's room that night with Berta. In fact, if George would agree, it'd be best to do that each night. He thought it wouldn't be wise to ask George now, though, because he could see that she was half sorry she'd made the offer to Joanna!

Julian was quite fussy that evening. He insisted on the blinds being drawn when they sat down to play cards after supper. He wouldn't let Berta take Sally out for a run, but took her himself, watching for any strange person as he went down the lane.

'You're making me feel quite scared!' said Anne with a laugh. 'Oh Ju, it's so hot in this room. Please, please let's have the blind up for a few minutes and let some air in. I'll begin to sizzle if we don't. Timmy would soon growl if there was anyone outside.'

'All right,' said Julian and drew up the blind. It was dark outside now, and the light streamed out.

'That's better,' said Anne, mopping her wet forehead. 'Now, whose turn is it? Yours, George.'

They sat around the table, playing. Julian and Berta sat side by side, as Julian was helping her learn the game. She looked exactly like a very earnest little boy, with her straight close-cut fair hair. George sat opposite the window with Dick on one side of her and Anne on the other.

'Your turn, Dick,' said George. 'Please hurry up, you're slow tonight.'

She sat and waited, looking out of the window into the darkness.

Then suddenly she slammed down her cards and leapt up, shouting. Everyone jumped almost out of their skins.

'What is it, what is it, George?' cried Julian.

'Out there – look – a face! I saw a face peering in at us – the light of the window just caught it! Timmy, Timmy! Quick, go after him!'

But Timmy wasn't there! Nor was Sally. George called frantically again. 'TIMMY! Come here, quickly. Oh no, that man'll get away. TIM!'

Timmy came bounding up the hall and into the sitting room, barking. Sally followed behind.

'Where were you! Idiot!' cried George furiously. 'Jump out of the window – go on – chase him, find him!'

Timmy leapt out of the window and Sally tried to do the same, but couldn't. She barked and yelped, trying again and again to jump out. Joanna came running in, panic-stricken, wondering what was happening.

'*Listen*,' said Julian, suddenly. 'Quiet, Sally. *Listen*!'

They were all suddenly quiet, Sally too. There

was the sound of a car being revved up down the lane, and then the sound died down as the car sped away.

'He's got away, whoever he was,' said Dick, and sat down suddenly. 'I feel as if I've been running a mile. You nearly scared the life out of me when you slammed down your cards like that, George, and yelled in my ear.'

Timmy leapt in at the window at that moment and Dick almost jumped out of his skin again. So did everyone else, including Sally, who fled behind the sofa in panic.

'*What's* all this about?' said Joanna, quite fiercely. 'Really!'

George was in a terrible rage – with Timmy! She shouted at the surprised dog and he put his tail down at once.

'Where were you? Why did you slink out of the room into the kitchen? How dare you leave me and go off like that? Just when we needed you! I'm ashamed of you, Timmy – you could have caught that man easily!'

'Oh don't,' said Berta, almost in tears. 'Poor Timmy! Don't, George!'

Then George turned on Berta. 'You just let me

tell off my own dog if he needs it! And you go and tell off yours too. I bet Timmy followed your horrible little woolly pet out into the kitchen – it was *her* fault, not his!'

'Be quiet, George,' said Julian. 'Your temper gets us nowhere. Calm down and let's hear what you saw. CALM DOWN.'

George stared at him, about to retort with something defiant. Then Timmy gave a small whimper – his heart was almost broken to hear George – George, his beloved mistress – rave at him in such anger. He had no idea what he'd done to displease her.

The whimper brought George to her senses.

'Oh Timmy!' she said, and knelt down and flung her arms around his neck. 'I didn't mean to shout at you. I was so angry because we missed our chance of getting that man who was peering in at us. Oh Timmy, it's all right, it really is.'

Timmy was extremely glad to hear it. He licked George lavishly, and then lay down by her. He wished he knew what all the excitement was about.

So did Joanna. She thumped on the table to get everyone's attention, and at last got Julian to explain everything to her. She stared out of the window, half thinking that she could see faces in the darkness outside. She drew the blind down sharply.

'We'll go to bed,' she said. 'All of us. I don't like this. I'll ring up the police and warn them. Lesley, you come with me straight away now.'

'I think you're right, Joanna,' said Julian. 'I'll lock up everywhere. Come on, everyone.'

Timmy was astonished and upset to find himself handed over to Joanna and Berta. Was George still cross with him then? It was a very, very long time since he'd slept away from her at night. He cheered up a little when he saw that Sally was going to be with him, and trotted rather mournfully up the attic stairs to Joanna's room.

Joanna soon got Berta into bed, and then undressed herself. She fastened the window and locked the door. She gave Timmy a rug in a corner, and Sally jumped up on Berta's bed as usual.

'Now we ought to be safe!' said Joanna, and settled creakingly into her bed.

On the floor below the two boys followed the same procedure, and so did Anne and George. Doors were locked and windows fastened,

although it was a hot night and they were all sure
they'd be melted by the morning. George couldn't
bear to think of Timmy with Berta and Joanna –
especially as she'd been so cross with him. She lay
in bed, full of remorse. Dear, kind, faithful Timmy
– how *could* she have shouted at him like that?

'Do you think Timmy's very upset?' she said,
when she and Anne were in bed.

'A bit, perhaps,' said Anne. 'But dogs are
very forgiving.'

'I know. That somehow makes it worse,'
said George.

'Well, you *shouldn't* get into such tempers,'
said Anne, seizing the opportunity to tell George
a few home truths. 'I thought you were getting
over the tantrums you used to have. But these
holidays you've been pretty bad. Because of
Berta, I suppose.'

'I wish I could go up and say good night
to Timmy,' George began again, after a few
minutes' silence.

'Oh for goodness' sake, George!' said Anne,
sleepily. 'Be sensible. You *can't* go and bang on
Joanna's door and ask for Timmy – you'd scare
them to death!'

Anne fell asleep, but George didn't. Then suddenly she heard the sound of a door being unlocked, and sat up. It sounded as if it came from the attic. Was it Joanna unlocking her door? What did she want?

A cautious little knock came at George's door.

'Who is it?' said George.

'Me. Joanna,' said Joanna's voice. 'I've brought Sally down, George. Timmy keeps trying to get up on Berta's bed to be with Sally, and she *can't* go to sleep, her camp bed's too small to hold all three of them. So will you have Sally, please?'

'Oh bother!' said George, and went to open her door. 'How's Timmy?' she said, in a low voice.

'All right,' said Joanna. 'He'll be annoyed I've taken Sally away. I'm glad to have him up there tonight with all these goings on!'

'Is he – is he happy, Joanna?' asked George, but Joanna had turned away and didn't hear.

George sighed. *Why* had she offered to let Joanna and Berta have Timmy tonight of all nights, when she had shouted at him so unfairly? Now she had to have this silly little Sally instead!

Sally whimpered. She didn't like being away

from Berta, and she wasn't fond of George. She wriggled out of George's arms and ran around the room, still whimpering.

Anne woke up with a jump.

'What's going on?' she said. 'Oh – it's Sally in the room! How did *she* get here?'

George told her, sounding very cross.

'Well, I hope she'll settle down,' said Anne. 'I don't want her to whimper and run around the bedroom all night long.'

But Sally wouldn't settle down. Her whimpering became louder, and when she took a flying jump on to George's bed and landed right on George's middle, the girl had had enough of it. She sat up and spoke in a fierce whisper.

'You silly dog! I'm going to take you downstairs and put you into Timmy's kennel!'

'Good idea,' said Anne, sleepily.

George picked up the lively little poodle and went out of the room, shutting the door softly. Anne promptly went to sleep again.

George crept down the stairs and went to the garden door. She undid it and walked out in dressing gown and pyjamas, her curly hair all tousled, carrying the whimpering little dog.

Suddenly she felt Sally stiffen in her arms, and growl. Grrrrrrr! George stood still. What had Sally heard?

Then things happened very suddenly indeed. A torch was flashed in her face, and before she could cry out, a cloth was thrown over her head so that she couldn't make a sound.

'This is the one!' said a low voice. 'The one with curly hair! And this is her dog, the poodle. Put him in that kennel, quick, before he barks the place down.'

Sally, too scared even to growl, was pushed into the kennel and the door shut on her. George, struggling and trying vainly to call out, was lifted off her feet and carried swiftly down to the front gate.

The garden door swung creaking to and fro in the night wind. Sally whimpered in her kennel. But no one heard either door or dog. Everyone in Kirrin Cottage was sound asleep!

# 14 Where is George?

Next morning, about half past seven, Joanna went downstairs as usual. Berta was awake and decided to fetch Sally from George's bedroom. She put on her dressing gown and padded downstairs with Timmy behind her, to George's room on the floor below. The door was shut, and she knocked gently.

'Come in,' said Anne's sleepy voice. 'Oh, it's you, Berta.'

'Yes. I've come for Sally,' said Berta. 'Hey – where's George?'

Anne looked at the empty bed beside hers. 'I don't know. The last thing I heard of her was in the middle of the night when we got cross because Sally wouldn't settle down, and George said she'd take her down to the kennel.'

'Oh. Well, probably George has gone down to fetch her back,' said Berta. 'I'll go up and dress. It's a gorgeous morning again. Are you going to swim before breakfast, because if so I'll just put on my swimming things.'

'Yes. I think we might today – we're nice and early,' said Anne, scrambling out of bed. 'Go and wake the boys. Timmy, go down and find George.'

Dick and Julian were awake, and ready for a before-breakfast swim. Anne joined them as they went downstairs. Berta had already gone down and had discovered Sally in the kennel, very excited to see her. She pranced around barking happily.

Timmy came up to the children, looking puzzled. He had hunted everywhere for George and hadn't found her. 'Woof,' he said to Anne. 'Woof, woof!' It was just as if he were saying, 'Please, where's George?'

'Haven't you found George yet?' said Anne in surprise. She called to Joanna. 'Joanna, where's George? Has she gone down to swim already?'

'I haven't seen her,' said Joanna. 'But I expect she has because the garden door was open when I came down, and I guessed one of you had gone for an early swim.'

'George must be down on the beach, then,' said

Anne, feeling rather puzzled.

Why hadn't George woken her and told her to come too?

Soon all four were on the beach with the two dogs, Sally very happy to be with Berta again, and Timmy very downcast and puzzled. He stood staring up the beach and down, looking completely lost.

'I can't see George anywhere,' said Dick, suddenly feeling scared. 'She's not in the sea.'

They all gazed over the water, but no one was swimming that morning. Anne turned to Julian in sudden panic.

'Ju! Where is she?'

'I wish I knew,' said Julian, anxiously. 'She's not here. And she hasn't gone out in her boat – it's over there. Let's go back to the house.'

'I don't think George would have gone for an early swim without telling me,' said Anne. 'And I think I'd have woken up just for a moment when she came back after taking Sally down – oh Julian, I think something happened when she went downstairs with Sally late last night!'

'I've been thinking that too,' said Julian. 'We know that there was someone around last night, because George saw a face outside the window. Let's go back to the house and see if we can spot anything to help us near the garden door or the kennel.'

They went back, looking very worried. As soon as they began to look about near the kennel, Anne gave an exclamation and bent down. She picked up something and held it out to the others without a word.

'What is it – oh, it's the cord off George's dressing gown!' said Dick, startled. 'That proves it! George was caught when she came down to put Sally into her kennel!'

'They must have thought she was *me*,' said Berta, in tears. 'She was carrying Sally and they know Sally belongs to me – and she has short hair too and dresses like a boy in the daytime.'

'That's it!' said Julian. 'Actually you *look* like a boy in your boys' things, but George doesn't – and the kidnappers are looking for a girl dressed as a boy – and George fitted the bill, especially as she had the poodle with her. She's been kidnapped!'

'And will my dad get the note to say his daughter won't be harmed if he does what the kidnappers want, and hands over this new secret?' said Berta.

'Sure to,' said Julian.

'What will they say when they know they've got George, not me?' asked Berta.

'Well . . .' said Julian, considering. 'I don't know. They might try the same thing with Uncle Quentin, but of course, he hasn't got the figures they want.'

'What about *Berta*?' asked Dick. 'As soon as those men find they've got the wrong girl, they'll be after Berta in a flash!'

'George won't tell them,' said Anne, at once. 'She'll know that Berta would be in danger if she did tell them – so she'll say nothing as long as she can.'

'Will she really?' said Berta, wonderingly. 'She's brave, isn't she? She could get herself set free at once if she said she wasn't me, and proved it. Gee, she's wunnerful if she could do a thing like that!'

'George is brave all right,' said Dick. 'As brave as anything when she's in trouble! Let's go and tell Joanna. We've GOT to decide what we're going to do about this – and also, we *have* to protect Berta somehow. She can't just wander around with us any more.'

Berta suddenly began to feel scared. George's sudden disappearance had brought home to her the very real danger she was in. She hadn't really believed in it before. She looked over her shoulder and all around as if she expected someone to pounce on her.

'It's all right, Berta – there's no one here now!' said Dick, comfortingly. 'But you'd better get indoors, all the same. I don't *think* George would give away the fact that she wasn't you, but the men might find out some other way – and then they'd come back!'

Berta raced indoors as if someone was chasing her! Julian shut and locked the garden door and called Joanna.

They had a very serious conference indeed. Joanna was horrified. She wept when she heard that George must have been kidnapped in the middle of the night. She wiped her eyes with her apron.

'I *said* we must lock the doors and the windows, I *said* we must tell the police – and then George has to go down all by herself into the garden!' she said. 'If only she hadn't had the poodle with her!

No wonder they thought she was Berta, with Sally in her arms.'

'Listen, Joanna,' said Julian. 'There are a lot of things to do. First we have to tell the police. Then somehow we have to contact Aunt Fanny and Uncle Quentin – it's typical of them not to give us an address! Then we have to decide about Berta. She has to be well hidden away somewhere.'

'Yes. Definitely,' said Joanna wiping her eyes again.

She sat and thought for a minute, and then her face lightened.

'I know where we could hide her!' she said. 'You remember Jo – the little traveller girl you've had one or two adventures with?'

'Yes,' said Julian. 'She lives with your cousin now, doesn't she?'

'She does,' said Joanna. 'And my cousin would have Berta straight away if she knew about this. She lives in a quiet little village where nothing ever happens, and nobody would think anything of my cousin having a child to stay with Jo. She often does.'

'It sounds like a good idea,' said Dick. 'Doesn't it, Julian? We've *got* to get Berta away right now.

We could trust Jo to look after her, too – Jo's as sharp as a packet of needles!'

'The police would know, too,' said Julian, 'and would keep an eye on her as well. Joanna, can you ring for a taxi and take Berta now, this minute?'

'It'll be a surprise for my cousin, my arriving this time of the morning,' said Joanna, standing up and taking off her apron, 'but she's quick on the uptake, and she'll do it, I know. Lesley, get a few things together.'

Berta looked extremely scared by now, and was inclined to refuse to go. Julian put his arm around her.

'Look,' he said, 'I bet George is holding her tongue so that we can get you away to safety before the men realise that they've got the wrong boy – so you can be brave, too, can't you?'

'Yes,' said Berta, looking up at Julian's kind, serious face. 'I'll do what you say – but what's this Jo like? I might not like her.'

'You'll like her,' said Julian. 'She's a scallywag – but her heart's in the right place – isn't it, Joanna?'

Joanna nodded. She had always been fond of

the reckless, cheeky little Jo, and it was she who had found a home for her when Jo's father had had to go to prison.

'Come on, Lesley,' she said. 'We must hurry. Julian, should she go as a girl or a boy now – we've got to decide that too.'

'A girl, please, please, a girl!' said Berta, at once.

Julian considered.

'Yes, I think you're right,' he said. 'You'd better be a girl now – but don't call yourself Berta yet.'

'She can be Jane,' said Joanna, firmly. 'That's a nice name, but ordinary enough for nobody to notice. Berta is too noticeable a name. Come along, now – we'll have to pick out your plainest clothes!'

'Now I'll call the police,' said Julian, 'and also order a taxi.'

'No, don't get a taxi for us,' said Joanna. 'I don't want to arrive at my cousin's little cottage in a taxi, and make everyone stare! Jane and I will catch the market bus and people will think I'm going off to market. We can get another bus there, that'll take us almost all the way to my cousin's. We've only got to walk down the lane then.'

'Good idea,' said Julian, and went to the phone.

He got hold of the police sergeant, and told his tale. The man showed no excitement but took down quickly all that Julian told him.

'I'll be up in ten minutes,' he said. 'Wait in till I come.'

Julian put down the receiver. Dick and Anne were watching him with troubled eyes. What was happening to George? Was she frightened – or furious – or perhaps hurt?

Timmy was absolutely miserable. He knew by now that something had happened to George. He'd gone a dozen times to the place where her dressing-gown cord had been found, and had sniffed around disconsolately.

Sally knew he was unhappy and trotted after him sadly. When he lay down she lay down beside him. When he got up, she got up too. It would have been amusing to watch if anyone had felt like being amused. But nobody felt that way!

Footsteps came up the path.

'The police!' said Julian. 'They've not been long!'

## 15  Discoveries in the wood

The sergeant had come and also a constable. Anne felt comforted when she saw the big, solid, responsible-looking men. Julian took them into the sitting room, and began to tell all that had happened.

In the middle of it there came the sound of footsteps racing down the stairs, and up the hall.

'We're just off!' shouted Joanna's voice. 'Can't stop to say goodbye, or we'll miss the bus!'

Down the garden path rushed Joanna, carrying a small suitcase of her own, which she had lent Berta, because Berta's was too expensive-looking. In it she had packed the very simplest of Berta's clothes, but secretly she had thought that she'd tell her cousin to dress Berta in some of Jo's things.

Berta ran behind her – a different Berta now, wearing a dress instead of jeans and jumper. She waved to the others as she went, trying to smile.

'I like Berta!' said Dick. 'She's not bad, that kid.'

'In fact, she's quite a honey!' said Julian, trying to make Anne smile.

'What's all that?' said the sergeant, in surprise, nodding his head towards the front path, down which Joanna and Berta had just rushed.

Julian explained. The sergeant frowned.

'You shouldn't have arranged that till you'd consulted us,' he said.

Julian was taken aback.

'Well, you see,' he said, 'it seemed to me that we should get Berta out of the house and hidden away at once in case the kidnappers realised quickly that they'd got the wrong girl.'

'That's true,' said the sergeant. 'Still, you *should* have consulted us. It seems quite a good idea to put her in that quiet village, with Jo to see to her – she's sharp, that Jo. I wouldn't put it past her to outwit the kidnappers any day! But this is a very serious business, you realise, Julian – it can't be dealt with by children.'

'Can you get George back?' asked Anne, breaking in with the question she'd been longing to ask ever since the police came.

'Maybe,' said the sergeant. 'Now I'll get in touch with your aunt and uncle, Julian, and with Mr Elbur Wright, and—'

The phone rang just then and Anne answered it.

'It's for you, Sergeant,' she said, and he took the phone from her.

'Ha. Hmm. Just so. Yes, yes. Right. Ha. Hmm.' The sergeant replaced the receiver and looked at Julian and the others. 'News has just come in that the kidnappers have contacted Mr Elbur Wright, and told him they've got his daughter Berta,' he said.

'Oh! And have they demanded that he tell them the secret figures he knows?' asked Julian.

The sergeant nodded. 'Yes. He's almost off his head with shock! He's promised to give them all they want. Very foolish!'

'You'd better tell him it's *not* Berta they've got, but George,' said Dick. 'Then he'll calm down!'

The sergeant frowned.

'Now, you leave this to *us*,' he said, ponderously. 'You'll only hinder us if you interfere or try meddling on your own. You just sit back and take things easy.'

'What! With George kidnapped and in danger?' exploded Dick. 'What are *you* going to do to get her back?'

'Now, now!' said the sergeant, annoyed. 'She's in no danger – she's not the person they want. They'll free her as soon as they realise that.'

'They won't,' said Dick. 'They'll get on to her dad and make *him* give up a few secrets!'

'Well, that'll give us a little more time to find these men,' said the irritating sergeant, and he stood up, big and burly in his navy blue uniform. 'Let me know *at once* if you have any other news, and please don't try to meddle. I assure you that we know the right things to do.'

He went out with the constable. Julian groaned. 'He doesn't see that this is *urgent*. It's so complicated too – the wrong girl kidnapped, the wrong father informed, the right one not at all inclined to give up powerful secrets – and poor George not knowing what's happening!'

'Thank goodness we got *Berta* out of the way,' said Dick. 'Anne, you look funny – are you all right?'

'Yes. I think I'm just shocked – and oh dear, I feel really *empty*!' said Anne, pressing her tummy.

'Oh – we forgot all about breakfast!' said Dick, staring at the clock. 'And it's almost ten o'clock now! What *have* we been doing all this time? Come on, Anne – let's get some food. We'll all feel better then.'

'I'm so sorry for poor Timmy and little Sally,' said Anne, as they went into the kitchen. 'Timmy, don't look at me like that! I don't know *where* your beloved George is, or I'd take you to her straight away! And Sally, you'll have to put up with me for a little while, because although I know where Berta is, I can't possibly take you there!'

They were soon sitting down to a plain breakfast of boiled eggs, toast and butter. It seemed strange only to be three. Dick tried to make conversation, but the other two were very quiet. Timmy sat under the table with his head on Anne's foot, and Sally stood beside her, paws on her knee. Anne comforted both the mournful dogs as best she could!

After they had cleared away breakfast, Anne went to make the beds, and the boys went outside to have another look at the place where George's dressing-gown cord had been found. Sally and

Timmy came with them.

Timmy sniffed around a lot, and then, nose to ground, went down the garden path to the front gate, and then pushed it open and went through it. Still nose to ground he went down the lane and turned off into a little path.

'Dick – he's following some kind of trail,' said Julian. 'I bet it's George's. Even if somebody *carried* her away, Timmy's clever enough to know George might be with him – he might just get a whiff of her.'

'Come on – let's follow Timmy,' said Dick, and the boys and Sally went along the little path, hot on Timmy's track.

Timmy began to run, and Dick called to him.

'Not so fast! We're coming too.'

But Timmy didn't slow down. Whatever it was he smelt, the scent was quite strong. The boys ran after him, beginning to feel excited.

But soon Timmy came to a full stop, in a little clearing in the wood. Dick and Julian panted up to where he was nosing around. He looked up at them forlornly. Evidently the scent came to an end there.

'Car tracks!' said Dick, pointing down to where

the dampish grass under a great oak tree had been rutted with big tyre-marks. 'See? The men brought a car here and hid it, then crept through the woods to Kirrin Cottage, and waited for a chance to get Berta. They got George instead – but they wouldn't have got *anyone* if only George hadn't been silly enough to take Sally to the kennel! The house was well and truly locked and bolted!'

Julian was looking at the wheel-tracks.

'These tracks were made by very big tyres,' he said. 'It was a car – and I think these are *American* tyre-marks. I can check that when I get back – I'll go and ask Jim at the local garage – he'll know. I'll just sketch one quickly.'

He took out a notebook and pencil and began to sketch. Dick bent down and looked more carefully at the tracks.

'There's quite a lot of criss-crossing of tracks,' he said. 'I think the men came here and waited. Then, when they got George, they must have pushed her into the car, and turned it to go back the way they came – see, the tracks lead down that wide path over there. They made a mess of the turning, though – bumped into this tree, look

– there's a mark right across it.'

'Where?' said Julian at once. 'Yes – a bright-blue mark – the car was that colour – or the wings were, at any rate. Well, that's something we've learnt! A big blue car, probably American. Surely the police could trace that?'

'Timmy's still nosing around, looking miserable,' said Dick. 'Poor Tim. I expect he knows George was pushed into a car just there. Hey – he's scraping at something!'

They ran to see what it was. Timmy was trying to get at some small object embedded in a car-rut. Evidently, in turning, the car had run over whatever it was.

Dick saw something broken in half – something green. He picked up the halves. 'A comb! Did George have a little green comb like this?'

'Yes. She did,' said Julian. 'She must have thrown it down when she got near to the car – to show us she was taken here – hoping we'd find it. And look, what's that?'

It was a handkerchief hanging on a gorse bush. Julian ran to it. It had the initial G on it in blue.

'Yes, it's George's,' he said. 'She's got six of these, all with different-coloured initials. She must have thrown this out too. Quick, Dick, look for anything else she might have thrown out of the car, while they were trying to turn it. They probably put her in the back, and she just had had a chance to throw out anything she had in her dressing-gown pocket, to let us know she was here if we came along this way.'

They searched for a long time. Timmy found one more thing, again embedded in a car-rut – a boiled sweet wrapped in cellophane paper.

'Look!' said Dick, picking it up. 'One of the sweets we all had the other night! George must have had one in her dressing-gown pocket! If only she'd had a pencil and bit of paper – she might have had time to write a note too!'

'That's an idea!' said Julian. 'Let's hunt again!'

But although they searched every bit of ground and every bush, there was no note to be found. It was too much to hope for!

'Let's just follow the car-tracks and make sure they reached the road,' said Julian.

So they followed them down the wide woodland path. At the side a little way along, a piece of paper blew in the wind, hopping an inch or two each time the breeze flapped it. Dick picked it up

– and then looked at Julian excitedly.

'She *did* have time to write a note! This is her writing. But there's only one word, look – what does it mean?'

Julian and Dick frowned over the piece of paper. Yes, it was George's writing – the G was exactly like the way she always wrote the big G at the beginning of her signature.

'Gringo,' read Julian. 'Just that one word. Gringo! What *does* it mean? It's something she heard them say, I suppose – and she just had time to write it and throw out the paper. Gringo! Timmy, what does *Gringo* mean?'

## 16 Jo!

Dick and Julian went back to Kirrin Cottage with the two disconsolate dogs. They showed Anne the things they had found, and she too puzzled over the word Gringo.

'We'll have to tell the police what you've discovered,' she said. 'They might trace the car, and they might know who or what Gringo is.'

'I'll phone them now,' said Julian. 'Dick, you go down to the garage with this sketch of the tyre-mark, and see if it's an American design.'

The police were interested but not helpful. The sergeant said he'd send his constable up to examine the place where the car had stood in the clearing, and gave it as his opinion that the bit of paper wasn't much use, as the boys had found it some way from the turning place of the car.

'Your cousin wouldn't be able to throw it out of the window once the car was going,' he said. 'There would be sure to be someone in the back with her. The only reason she could throw things out at the clearing would be because the second man – and there would certainly be two – would be guiding the other man in the turning of the car.'

'The wind might have blown the note along the path,' said Julian. 'Anyway, I've given you the information.'

It was a very miserable day, although the sun shone down warmly, and the sea was blue and very inviting. But nobody wanted to swim, nobody really wanted to do anything but talk and talk about George and what had happened, and where she could be at that moment!

Joanna came back in time to get their lunch, and was pleased to find that Anne and Julian had done the potatoes and prepared a salad, and that Dick had managed to pick some raspberries. They were very glad to see Joanna. She was someone sensible and comforting and matter-of-fact.

'Well, Jane is now safely in my cousin's cottage,' she said. 'She was very miserable but I told her she must smile and play about, or else the neighbours would wonder about her. I put her into some of Jo's clothes – they fitted her all right.

Hers are too expensive-looking, and would make people talk!'

They told Joanna what they'd discovered in the clearing that morning. She took the note and looked at it.

'Gringo!' she said. 'That's a funny word – sounds like a traveller word to me. It's a pity Jo isn't here – she might be able to tell us what it means!'

'Did you see Jo?' asked Dick.

'No. She was out shopping,' said Joanna, lifting the lid to look at the potatoes. 'I hope she gets on with Jane all right. Really, it's getting very difficult to remember that child's change of names!'

The only fresh news that day was a worried phone call from Aunt Fanny. She was shocked and amazed at the news she had heard.

'Your uncle has collapsed!' she said. 'He's been working very hard, you know, and now this news of George has been the last straw. He's very ill. I can't leave him at the moment – but anyway we couldn't do anything! Only the police can help now. To think those horrible men took George by mistake!'

'Don't worry too much, Aunt Fanny,' said

Julian. 'We've hidden Berta away safely, and I expect the men will free George as soon as she tells them she's the wrong girl.'

'If she *does* tell them!' said Dick, under his breath. 'She might not, for Berta's sake, for a few days at any rate!'

Everyone went to bed that night feeling miserable. Anne took Timmy and Sally with her, for both were so forlorn that she couldn't bear to do anything else. Timmy wouldn't eat anything at all, and Anne was worried about him.

Julian couldn't go to sleep. He tossed and turned, thinking about George. Hot-tempered, courageous, impatient, independent George! He worried and worried about her, wishing he could *do* something!

A small stone suddenly rattled against his window! He sat up, alert at once. Then something fell right into the room, and rolled over the floor. Julian was at the window in a trice. Who was throwing pebbles at his window?

He leaned out. A voice came up to him at once. 'Is it you, Dick?'

'Jo! What *are* you doing here?' said Julian, startled. 'It's Julian. Dick's asleep. I'll wake him, and let you in.'

But he didn't need to go down and let Jo in. She was up a tree outside the window and across some ivy and on his windowsill before he had even shaken Dick awake!

She slid into the room. Julian switched on his light. There was Jo, sitting at the end of Dick's bed, the familiar cheeky grin on her face! She was very brown, but still showed her freckles, and her hair was as short and curly as ever.

'I *had* to come,' she said. 'When I got home from shopping, there was this girl Jane. She told me all about how George had been mistaken for her and kidnapped – and when I said to her, "You go straight away and say it's all a mistake, and George has got to be set free!" she wouldn't! She just wouldn't! All she did was to sit and cry. Little coward!'

'No, Jo,' said Dick, and tried to explain everything to the indignant girl.

But he couldn't convince her.

'If I was that girl Jane I wouldn't let someone stay kidnapped because of me,' she said. 'I don't like her, she's silly. And I'm supposed to keep an eye on her! Ha! Not me! I'd *like* her to be kidnapped, the way she's behaving about George.'

Julian looked at Jo. She was very, very loyal to the Five, and proud of being their friend. She had been in two adventures with them now, a clever little traveller girl, and a very loyal friend. Her father was in prison, and she was living with a cousin of Joanna's, and, for the first time in her life, going to school!

'Listen, Jo – we've found out a few more things since Berta – I mean Lesley – no, I don't, I mean Jane . . .'

'What *do* you mean?' said Jo, puzzled.

'I mean Jane,' said Julian. 'We've found out something else since Joanna parked Jane with her cousin this morning.'

'Go on, tell me,' said Jo. 'Have you found out where George is? I'll go and break in and get her out, if you have!'

'Oh Jo – it's no use just being fierce,' said Dick. 'Things aren't as easy as that!'

'George threw out a bit of paper with this written on it,' said Julian, and he put it in front of Jo. 'See? Just that one word – "Gringo". Does it mean anything to you?'

'Gringo?' said Jo. 'That rings a bell! Let's

see now – *Gringo*!'

She frowned as she thought hard. Then she nodded. 'Oh yes, I remember now. A fair came to the town a few weeks back – the big town not far from our village. It was called Gringo's Great Fair.'

'Where did it go?' asked Dick, eagerly.

'It was going to Fallenwick, then to Granton,' said Jo. 'I made friends with the boy whose dad owned the merry-go-round, and I had about a hundred free rides.'

'You *would*!' said both boys together, and Jo grinned.

'Do you think this Gringo, who runs the fair, could be anything to do with the name Gringo that George wrote on this paper?' said Julian.

'*I* dunno!' said Jo. 'But if you like I can go and find the fair and get hold of Spiky – that's the merry-go-round boy – and see if I can find out anything. I know Spiky said Gringo was a real horror to work for!'

'Did he have a big American car?' asked Dick, suddenly.

'I dunno that either,' said Jo. 'I can find out. Here – I'll go *now*! You lend me a bike and I'll bike to Granton!'

'No chance,' said Julian, startled at the idea of Jo biking the twelve miles to Granton in the middle of the night.

'All right,' said Jo, rather sulkily. 'I just thought you'd like me to help. It might be that this Gringo has got George somewhere. He was the kind of man who was a go-between, if you know what I mean.'

'How?' asked Dick.

'Well, Spiky said that if anyone wanted something dirty done, this Gringo just held out his hand, and if a wad of notes was put into it, he'd do it, and nothing said!' said Jo.

'I see,' said Julian. 'Hmm – it sounds as if kidnapping would be right up his street, then.'

Jo laughed scornfully. 'That'd be nothing to him – chicken-feed. Come on, Julian – let me borrow your bike.'

'NO,' said Julian. 'Thanks very, very much, but I'm not letting anyone ride to a fair in the middle of the night to find out if a man called Gringo has anything to do with George. I can't believe he has, either – it's too far-fetched.'

'All right. But you *asked* me if the name meant

anything to me,' said Jo, sounding offended. 'Anyway, it's a common enough nickname in the circus world and the fair world too. There's probably a thousand Gringos about!'

'It's time you went back home,' said Julian, looking at his watch. 'And be nice to Berta – I mean Jane – *please*, Jo. You can come over tomorrow to see if there's any more news. How did you get here tonight, by the way?'

'Walked,' said Jo. 'Well – ran, I mean. Not by the roads, though – they take too long. I go like the birds do – as straight as I can, and it's *much* shorter!'

Dick had a sudden picture of the brave little Jo speeding through woods and fields, over hills and through valleys, as straight as a crow flying homewards. How did she find her way like that? He knew *he'd* never be able to!

Jo slipped out over the windowsill, and down the tree, as easily as a cat.

'Bye!' she said. 'See you soon.'

'Give our love to Jane,' whispered Dick.

'Won't!' said Jo, much too loudly, and disappeared.

Julian switched out the light.

'Whew!' he said, 'I always feel as if I've been blown about by a strong, fresh wind when I see Jo. What a girl! Imagine wanting to ride all the way to Granton tonight, after running all the way here from Berta's!'

'Yes. I'm glad you wouldn't let her take your bike,' said Dick. 'It's a good thing she wouldn't dare to disobey you!'

He got into bed – and just at that very moment the two boys heard a loud ringing noise. Dick sat up straight away.

'I don't believe it!' he said.

'What's up?' said Julian, and then he too realised what the ringing was – a bicycle bell. Yes, a bell rung loudly and defiantly by someone cycling swiftly along the sea road towards Granton!

'It's *Jo*!' said Dick. 'And she's taken my bike! I know its bell. Oh, just wait till I get hold of her!'

Julian gave a loud laugh. 'She's a monkey, a brave, loyal, aggravating *monkey*. What a cheek she's got! She didn't dare to take *my* bike when I'd said no – so she took yours. Well – we can't do a thing about it now. What that merry-go-round boy is going to think when he's woken in the middle of the night by Jo, I cannot imagine.'

'He's probably used to her,' said Dick. 'Well, let's go to sleep. I wonder if George is asleep or awake? I hate to think of her a prisoner somewhere.'

'I bet Timmy hates it more than we do,' said Dick, hearing a long-drawn whimper from the next room. 'Poor Tim. He can't go to sleep either!'

Dick and Julian managed to go to sleep at last, both thinking of a speedy little figure on a bike, racing through the night to ask questions of a merry-go-round boy called Spiky!

# 17  To Gringo's Fair

At half past seven next morning Joanna came running upstairs to Julian's bedroom, a piece of paper in her hand. She knocked on the door.

'Julian! A little note was on the front-door mat when I got down this morning. It's folded over with your name on the outside.'

Julian was out of bed in a trice. A note from the kidnappers perhaps? No – it couldn't be. They wouldn't write to *him*!

It was from Jo! She had scribbled it so badly that Julian could hardly read it.

'Julian, I saw Spiky, he's coming to the beach at eleven. I took Dick's bike to go home on. I'll bring it back at eleven, don't be too cross. Jo.'

'Little monkey,' said Dick. 'I hope she hasn't damaged my bike.'

Jo hadn't. She had actually managed to find time to clean it before she left home, and arrived with it so bright and gleaming that Dick hadn't the heart to scold her!

She was early so she came to the house instead of the beach. She rode through the gate and up the front path and Timmy ran to greet her with a volley of delighted barks. He liked Jo – in fact he really loved the little girl. She certainly had a way with animals! Sally followed, dancing on her tiptoes as usual, ready to welcome as a friend anyone that Timmy liked.

Dick hailed Jo from the front door as she came up. 'Hello, bike-stealer! Hey, what's happened to my bike – have you spring-cleaned it?'

Jo grinned, looking at Dick warily. 'Yes. I'm sorry I took it, Dick.'

'You're not a bit sorry – but I'll forgive you,' said Dick, grinning too. 'So you got to the fair safely after all?'

'Oh yes – and I woke up Spiky – he was really surprised,' said Jo. 'But his dad was sleeping in the same caravan as he was, so I couldn't say much. I just told him to be on Kirrin Beach at eleven. Then I rode back home. I ought to have left your bike on the way back, but I was a bit tired, so I rode home, instead of walking.'

'You can't have had much sleep last night,' said

Julian, looking at the sunburnt girl with her untidy curly hair. 'Hey – who's that?'

A short, plump boy was hurrying past the gate. He had a mop of black hair which stuck up into strange spikes of hair at the crown.

'Oh – that's Spiky!' said Jo. 'He's on time, isn't he? He's called Spiky because of his hair. You won't believe it, but he spends a fortune on hair-gel, trying to make those spiky bits go flat. But they won't.'

She called loudly.

'Spiky! Hey, SPIKY!'

Spiky turned at once. He had a pleasant, rather lopsided face, and eyes as black as currants. He stood staring at Jo and the boys.

'I'm just off to the beach,' he said.

'Right. We're coming too,' said Jo, and she and the boys went to join him.

They met the ice-cream man on the way and Julian bought an ice-cream for each of them.

'Thanks,' said Spiky, pleased.

He was a bit shy of Dick and Julian, and wondered very much why he'd been asked to come.

They sat down on the beach.

'I was scared when you came tapping at the window last night,' he said to Jo, licking his ice-cream with a very pink tongue. 'What's it all about?'

'Well,' said Julian, cautiously, 'we're interested in somebody called Gringo.'

'Old Gringo?' said Spiky. 'A lot of people are interested in Gringo. Do you know what we say at the fair? We say Gringo ought to put up a notice. "All dirty work done here!" He's bad, Gringo is – but he pays us well, even if he works us hard.'

'He owns the fair, doesn't he?' said Julian, and Spiky nodded. 'I expect he uses it as a cover for all his other, bigger jobs,' Julian said to Dick.

He looked at the plump, black-eyed boy, wondering how far he could trust him. Jo saw the look and knew what it meant.

'He's all right,' she said, nodding towards Spiky. 'You can say what you like. He's an oyster, he is. Aren't you, Spiky?'

Spiky grinned his lopsided grin. Julian decided to trust him, and speaking in a low voice that really thrilled Spiky, he told him about the kidnapping of George. Spiky's eyes nearly fell out of his head.

'I bet old Gringo's at the bottom of that,' he said. 'Last week he went off up to London – he told my dad he was on to a big job – an American job, he said it was.'

'Yes – it sounds as if it all fits,' said Julian. 'Spiky, this kidnapping happened the night before last. Did anything unusual happen in the fair camp, do you know? It would have been in the middle of the night.'

Spiky considered. He shook his head. 'No – I don't think so. Gringo's big double caravan is still there – so he can't have gone. He had it moved right away from the camp yesterday morning – said there was too much noise for his old mum, who lives in his posh caravan and looks after him. We were all glad it was moved – now he can't spy on us so easily!'

'I suppose you—' began Julian, and then stopped as Dick gave an exclamation.

'I've got an idea!' he said. 'What if that caravan was moved for *another* reason – what if someone was making a noise inside the van – someone shouting for help, say! Gringo would have to move it away from the rest of the camp in case that someone was heard.'

There was a pause, and then Spiky nodded. 'Yes. It could be,' he said. 'I've never known Gringo move his caravan away from the camp before. Shall I do a bit of spying for you?'

'Yes,' said Julian, excited. 'It'd be brilliant if we could find George so quickly – and so near us too! A fair camp would be a wonderful place to hide her, of course. Thank goodness we found that bit of paper with "Gringo" written on it!'

'Let's all go to the fair this afternoon,' said Dick. 'Timmy too. He'd smell out George at once.'

'Hadn't we better tell the police first?' said Julian.

At once Spiky and Jo got up in alarm. Spiky looked as if he were going to run away immediately!

'Don't you get the police, Julian!' said Jo urgently. 'You won't get anything more out of Spiky, if you do. Not a thing.'

'I'm going,' said Spiky, still looking terrified.

'No you're not,' said Dick, and caught hold of him. 'We won't go to the police. They might frighten off Gringo and make him smuggle George away at once. I bet he has plans to do that anyway.

We won't say a word, so sit down and be sensible.'

'You can believe him,' Jo told Spiky. 'He's straight, OK?'

Spiky sat down, still looking wary.

'If you're coming to the fair, come at four,' he said. 'It's half-day closing today for the towns around, and the place'll be packed. If you want to do any looking around, you won't be noticed in that crowd.'

'Right,' said Julian. 'We'll be there. Look out for us, Spiky, in case you've got any news.'

Spiky then left, and the boys couldn't help smiling at his back view – the spikes of hair at the top of his head were very noticeable!

'You'd better stay to lunch with us, Jo,' said Dick, and the delighted girl beamed all over her face.

'Will Joanna's cousin mind you not being back to lunch?' asked Julian.

'No. I said I wouldn't be back all day,' said Jo. 'It's still school holidays, you see. Anyway, I can't stand that Jane – she mopes around all the time – and she's got some of my clothes on, too.'

Jo sounded so indignant about Berta that the

boys had to laugh. They all went back to Kirrin Cottage, and found Joanna and Anne hard at work in the house.

'You monkey!' said Joanna to Jo. 'Up to your usual tricks, I hear. Throwing stones at people's windows in the middle of the night. You just try that on *my* window and see what happens to you! Now, put on that apron, and help around a bit. How's Jane?'

Joanna was very excited to hear about the boys' latest ideas as to where George might be. Julian gave her a warning.

'But no ringing up the police behind our backs *this* time, Joanna,' he said. 'This is something best done by Dick and me.'

'Can I come with Sally?' asked Anne.

'We can't *possibly* take Sally,' said Dick, 'in case Gringo's about and recognises her. So you'd better stay and look after her, and we'll take Timmy. He'd be sure to smell where George is, if she's hidden anywhere in the camp. But I think she's probably in Gringo's own caravan.'

Timmy pricked up his ears every time he heard George's name mentioned. He was a very miserable dog indeed, and kept running to the front gate, hoping to see George coming along. Whenever they missed him, they knew where to find him – lying mournfully on George's empty bed – probably with an equally mournful Sally beside him!

The boys and Jo set off to the fair about half past three, on their bikes. Jo rode Anne's this time, and Timmy ran valiantly beside them. Jo glanced at Dick's bike from time to time, proud of its shine – she had cleaned it well that morning!

They came to the fair. 'You can put your bikes up against Spiky's caravan,' said Jo. 'They'll be safe there. Will you pay, and then we'll get in straight away? You needn't pay for me – I'm going through the gap in the hedge. I'm Spiky's friend, so it's all right.'

She gave Dick her bike and disappeared. Julian paid and went in at the gate. They saw Jo waving wildly to them from the side of the big field and wheeled the three bikes over to her. Timmy followed closely at their heels.

'Hello!' said Spiky, appearing suddenly. 'I've got to go and run the merry-go-round. I've got a bit of news, but not much. That's Gringo's caravan over there, the double one, big van in front, little van behind.'

He nodded his head to where a magnificent caravan stood, right away from the rest of the camp. There were people milling about all around the other vans, but there was nobody at all by Gringo's. Evidently no one dared to go too near.

'Let's buy a ball at one of the stands, and then go and play near Gringo's caravan,' said Dick, in a low voice. 'Then one of us will throw the ball too hard and it'll go near the van – and we'll somehow manage to get a look inside. Timmy can go sniffing around while we play. If George is there he'll bark the place down.'

'Good idea!' said Julian. 'Come on, Jo! And keep your eyes open all the time in case you've got to warn us of danger.'

## 18  Spiky is very helpful

The two boys and Jo, with Timmy at their heels, wandered around the fair to find somewhere to buy a ball. There seemed to be none for sale, so they had a go at a hoopla stall, and Julian managed to get a ring around a small red ball. Perfect!

It was a big and noisy fair, and hundreds of people from the nearby towns had come on the shops' early-closing day to enjoy the fun. The merry-go-round played its loud, raucous music all the time, swings went to and fro, the dodgem cars banged and bumped one another as usual, and sellers went around shouting their wares.

'Balloons! Giant balloons!'

'Ice-cream! All flavours.'

'Tell your fortune, lady? I'll tell it true as can be!'

Jo was very much at home in the fair. She had been brought up in one, and knew all the tricks of the trade. Timmy was amazed at the noise, and kept close to the boys, his tail still down because he couldn't forget that George was missing.

'Now let's play our little game of ball,' said Julian. 'Come on, Tim – and if we get into any trouble, just growl and show your teeth, OK?'

The three of them, with Timmy, went to the clear space of field that separated the magnificent caravan from the rest of the camp. A man at a nearby stall called to them.

'Hey! You'll get into trouble if you play there!' But they took no notice and he shrugged his shoulders and began to shout his wares.

They threw the ball to one another, and then Julian flung it so wildly that it ran right up to the wheels of the front caravan of the pair. In a trice Dick and Jo were after it. Jo leapt up on a wheel and looked in at the big window, while Dick ran to the small van that was attached behind the big one.

A quick glance assured Jo that the big caravan was empty. The interior was furnished in a very luxurious way and looked like a very good bedsit. She leapt down.

Dick peered into the window of the smaller van. At first he thought there was no one there –

and then he saw a pair of very fierce, angry eyes looking at him – the eyes of a small, bent old woman. She was sitting sewing on a bunk, and, as he looked in, she shook her fist at him and called out something he couldn't hear.

He jumped down and joined the others. 'No one at all in the big van,' said Jo.

'Only an old woman in the other,' reported Dick, in deep disappointment. 'Unless George is pushed under a bunk or squashed into a cupboard, she's not there!'

'Timmy doesn't seem interested in the caravans at all, does he?' said Julian. 'I'm sure if George really *was* in one of those caravans, he'd bark and try to get inside.'

'Yes – I think he would,' said Dick. 'Hey, there's somebody coming out of the second van. It's the old lady! She's in a terrible temper!'

So she was! She came down the steps to the van, shouting and shaking her fist at them. 'Tim – go and find, go and find – in that van!' said Julian, suddenly, as the woman came towards them.

The three of them stood their ground as the woman came right up. They couldn't understand a word she said, partly because she had no teeth, and partly because she spoke a mixture of many languages. Anyway, it was obvious that she was telling them off for daring to play near the two vans.

Timmy had understood what Julian had said, and had slipped inside the second van. He was there for half a minute, and then he barked. The boys jumped, and Dick made a move towards the van.

Then Timmy appeared, dragging something behind him with his teeth. He tried to bark at the same time, but he couldn't. He dragged the coat-like thing right down to the ground before the old woman was on him, screaming in a high voice, and hitting him. She pulled the garment away and went up the steps, kicking out at the surprised Timmy as he tried to pull it away. The door slammed.

'If that woman hadn't been old, Timmy would have soon shown her he was top dog!' said Dick. 'What was he pulling out of the van?'

'Come over here, out of sight of the van,' said Julian, urgently. 'Didn't you recognise it, Dick? It was *George's dressing gown*!'

'Oh!' said Dick, stopping in surprise. 'Yes,

you're right – it was. What does that mean exactly? George definitely isn't in those vans, or Timmy would have found her.'

'I sent him in to see if he could *smell* that George had been hidden there,' said Julian. 'I thought he'd bark excitedly if he smelt her scent anywhere – on the bunk, perhaps. I never guessed he'd find her *dressing gown* and drag it out to show us!'

'Good Timmy! Clever Timmy!' said Dick, patting the dog, whose tail was now at half mast instead of right down. He had at least found George's dressing gown – but how surprising to find it in that caravan!

'Why on earth didn't they take the dressing gown with them, when they took George off?' wondered Julian. 'She's definitely *been* in that caravan – she was taken straight there the night before last, I expect. Where is she now?'

'She must have been dressed differently,' said Dick. 'They must have had to dress her properly, when they took her somewhere else. After all, she was only in pyjamas and dressing gown.'

Jo was listening to all this, puzzled and worried. She nudged Dick. 'Spiky's beckoning to us,' she said.

They went over to the merry-go-round boy, whose father was now in charge of the noisy machine.

Spiky took them into his caravan, a small one, in which he lived with his father.

'I saw Gringo's old mum chasing you!' he said with his lopsided grin. 'What was your dog dragging out of the van?'

They told him. He nodded.

'I've been asking around a bit, quietly,' he said, 'just to see if anyone had heard anything from Gringo's caravan – and the man whose caravan is nearest told me he heard shouts and yells two nights ago. He reckoned it was someone in Gringo's van – but he's too scared of Gringo to go and interfere, of course.'

'That'd be George yelling,' said Dick.

'Well, then Gringo's vans were moved the next day right away from the other vans,' said Spiky. 'And this afternoon, before the fair opened, Gringo got his car and towed the little van – the second one – out of the field, and set off with it. We all wondered why, but he told somebody it needed repairing.'

'And George was inside!' said Dick. 'Clever

way of moving her off to another hiding place.'

'When did the van come back?' asked Julian.

'Just before you came,' said Spiky. 'I don't know where it went. It was gone an hour, I should think.'

'An hour,' said Dick. 'Well, say it goes at an average of 25 miles an hour – you can't go very fast if you're towing something – that'd mean he'd gone somewhere about 12 miles or so away, and come back the same distance – making about an hour's drive, allowing for a stop when they arrived at the place they had to leave her at.'

'Yes,' said Julian. 'But there are lots of places within the radius of 12 miles!'

'Where's Gringo's *car*?' said Dick suddenly.

'Over there, under that big tarpaulin,' said Spiky. 'It's a silver-grey American one – very big. He thinks the world of it, Gringo does.'

'I'm going to have a look at it,' said Julian, and strode off.

He came to the tarpaulin, which covered the car right to the ground. He lifted it and was just about to look under it when a man ran up, shouting.

'Here, you! Leave that alone! You'll be turned

out of the fair if you mess about with things that are none of your business!'

But Timmy was with Julian, and he turned and growled so fiercely that the man stopped in a hurry. Julian had plenty of time to take a good look under the tarpaulin!

Yes – the car was silver-grey, a big American one – and the wings were bright blue! Julian took a quick look at the two left-hand ones and saw a deep scratch on one of them. Before he dropped the tarpaulin he had time to glance at the tyres. He was sure they had the same pattern as those shown in the wheel-tracks he'd sketched! He had checked the sketch with Jim, at Kirrin Garage, who had told him they were an American design.

Yes – this was the car that had hidden in the clearing the night before last – the car that had turned with difficulty and made those deep ruts – the car that had taken George away, and this afternoon had towed away the caravan with her inside, to hide her somewhere else.

He dropped the tarpaulin and walked back to the others, excited, taking no notice of the rude things that the nearby man called out to him.

'It's the car, all right,' said Julian. 'Now – WHERE did it go this afternoon? If only we could find out!'

'It's such a fantastic car that anyone would notice it – especially as it was towing a nice little caravan,' said Dick.

'Yes – but we can't go around the countryside asking everyone we meet if they've noticed a silver-grey car with blue wings,' said Julian.

'Let's go back home and get a map and look at the country around about,' said Dick. 'Spiky, which way did the car turn when it went out of the field gate?'

'Towards the east,' said Spiky. 'On the road to Big Twillingham.'

'Well, that's useful to know,' said Dick. 'Come on, let's get our bikes. Thanks a lot, Spiky. You've been a big help. We'll let you know what happens.'

'Call on me if ever you want more help,' said Spiky, proudly, and gave them a little salute, bobbing his head so that his spikes of hair shook comically.

The three of them rode off, with Timmy running beside them again. As soon as they got home they told Anne and Joanna all they had found out. Joanna was for ringing up the police at once again, but Julian stopped her.

'I think we can do this next bit of work better than they can,' he said. 'We're going to try and find out where the car went, Joanna. Now – where are the maps of the district?'

They found them and began to pore over them. Jo was completely lost when it came to map reading. She could find her way anywhere, day or night – but not with a map!

'Now – here's the road to Big Twillingham and Little Twillingham,' Julian said. 'Let's list all the roads the car could take from there. This is going to take a while!'

## 19 An exciting plan

After fifteen minutes they had six towns on their list, all of which could have been reached in about half an hour from Big Twillingham, which was two miles away from the fair.

'And *now* what do you want to do, Ju?' asked Dick. 'Bike over to all the towns and ask if anyone has seen the car?'

'No. We can't do that,' said Julian. 'I'm going down to the garage to see our friend Jim, and get *his* help! I'm going to ask him to ring up any friends he has in the garages in those towns, and ask if they've seen the car passing through.'

'Won't he think it's a bit funny?' asked Anne.

'Yes. But he won't mind how funny it is if we pay for the phone calls and give him some money for his trouble!' said Julian, folding up the map. 'And he won't ask any questions either. He'll probably think it's some silly bet we've got on.'

Jim was happy to ring up the garages for

them. He knew boys working in main garages in four of the towns, and he knew the hall porter of a hotel in the fifth town. But he knew no one in the sixth.

'That doesn't matter!' he said. 'We'll ring up the garage in the High Street there, and just ask whoever comes to the phone.'

Jim rang up the garage in Hillingford, and had a jokey conversation with his friend there. He put the phone down.

'It's a no,' he said. 'He says no car like that came through Hillingford, or he'd have noticed it that time of day. I'll ring up Jake at Green's Garage in Lowington now.'

'That's a no as well,' he said, after a minute's phone conversation. 'I'll try my hall porter now. He's a cousin of mine.'

The hall porter had some news.

'Yes!' Jim kept saying. 'Yes, that's the one! Yes, yes! You heard him say that, did you? Thanks a lot.'

'What is it?' asked Dick, eagerly, when Jim at last put down the phone.

'Pat – that's the hall porter – says he was off duty this afternoon, and went to buy some cigarettes at a little shop in the main street of Graysfield, where his hotel is – and as he stood talking to the man in the shop an enormous car drew up at the kerb – silver-grey, with blue wings – an American car, left-hand drive and all.'

'Yes – what next?' said Julian, eagerly.

'Well, the driver got out to get some cigarettes at the shop. He had sunglasses on, and a big gold ring on his finger – Pat noticed that . . .'

'That must be the man who asked about us at the café in Kirrin!' said Julian, remembering. 'Go on, Jim – this is wonderful!'

'Well, Pat's interested in big cars, so he went out and had a good look at it,' said Jim. 'He said the car had its blinds drawn down at the back, so he couldn't see inside. The man with the sunglasses came out and got into the driver's seat again. He called out to whoever was behind and said "Which way now?"'

'Yes, yes – did he hear the answer?' said Julian.

'Somebody called back and said, "Not far now. Into Twining, turn to the left, and it's the house on the hill."'

'*Well*! That's lucky!' said Dick. 'Would that be

where G—' He stopped at a sharp nudge from
Julian, and remembered that he mustn't give too
much away to the helpful Jim.

Julian gave some money to the pleased garage
boy, who pocketed it at once, grinning.

'You just come along to me if you want to know
about any more cars,' he said. 'I'll phone all over
the place for you! Thanks a lot!'

They sped back to Kirrin Cottage, too excited
even to talk. They flung their bikes against the
wall and ran in to tell Anne and Joanna. Timmy
and Sally sensed their excitement and danced
around, barking loudly.

'We know where George is!' cried Dick. 'We
know, we know!'

Joanna and Anne listened eagerly.

'Well, Julian,' said Joanna, in admiration, 'it
was really clever of you to make Jim phone up
like that. The police couldn't have done better.
What are you going to do now? Ring up that
sergeant?'

'No,' said Julian. 'I'm so afraid that if the police
get moving on this now, they'll alarm Gringo and
he'll take George away somewhere else. Dick and
I will go to this place tonight, and see if we can

get hold of George and bring her back! After all – it's only an ordinary house, I expect – and Gringo doesn't think that anyone knows where George is, so he won't be on the lookout!'

'Good!' said Dick. 'Good, good, good!'

'I'm coming too,' said Jo.

'You're not,' said Julian, at once. 'That's flat – you're NOT COMING, Jo. But I'll take Timmy, of course.'

Jo said no more, but looked so sulky that Anne laughed. 'Cheer up, Jo. You can keep me and Sally company. Oh Julian – wouldn't it be *wonderful* to find George and rescue her!'

There was more map reading as the boys decided which was the best way to bike over to Graysfield.

'Find the best torches we've got, Anne, will you?' said Dick. 'And how can we bring George back once we've got her? On the back of my bike, I think, although I know it's not allowed. But this is very urgent. We can't take a third bike with us. Isn't this exciting!'

'We really ought to ring up the police,' said Joanna, who kept saying this at intervals.

'Joanna, you sound like a parrot!' said Julian.

'If we're not back by morning you can ring up all the police in the country if you want to!'

'There's been another phone call from your aunt today, Julian – I nearly forgot to tell you,' said Joanna. 'Your uncle's better and they're coming home as soon as possible.'

'Not this evening, I hope,' said Julian, in alarm. 'Did they tell you anything about Mr Wright – Berta's dad?'

'Oh, he's hanging on to his secrets happily now that he knows it isn't Berta who's kidnapped,' said Joanna. 'I don't know if the kidnappers even know they've got the wrong girl yet. It's all very hush-hush. Even your uncle and aunt are having to obey the police. Your poor aunt's terribly upset about George.'

'Yes. She must be really worried,' said Julian. 'We've had so much excitement today that I've almost forgotten to worry. And anyway when you're able to *do* something, things don't seem so bad.'

'Don't go and do too much and get yourself in trouble,' said Joanna, darkly.

'I'll be careful!' said Julian, winking at Dick. 'Hey – isn't it nearly supper-time? I'm really hungry.'

'Well, we haven't had any tea. No wonder we're hungry.'

'Would you like bacon and eggs for a treat?' said Joanna, and there was a chorus of approval at once.

Timmy and Sally wagged their tails as if Joanna's question applied to them too!

'We'll set off as soon as it's dark,' said Julian. 'Jo, you'd better go home after supper. They'll be worrying about you.'

'All right,' said Jo, pleased to have been asked to supper, but still sulky at being forbidden to go with Julian and Dick that night.

Jo disappeared after supper, with many messages to Berta from Dick, Julian, Anne and Sally.

'And I bet she doesn't give a single one of them!' said Dick. 'Let's have a game before we set off, Julian. Just to take our minds off the excitement. I'm getting all worked up!'

Joanna went up to bed at ten because she was tired. Anne stayed up to see the boys off.

'You *will* be careful,' she kept saying. 'You *will* be careful, won't you? I think it's almost worse to stay behind and wonder what's happening to you, than to go with you and find out!'

At last the time came for the boys to go. It was a quarter to twelve and, except for a small moon, it was a dark night, with great clouds looming up, often hiding the moon.

'Come on, Timmy,' said Dick. 'We're going to find George.'

'Woof!' said Timmy, delighted. Sally wuffed too, and was very disappointed at being left behind. The boys wheeled their bikes to the front gate.

'See you, Anne!' said Dick. 'Go to bed – and hope to see George when you wake up!'

They set off on their bikes, with Timmy loping along beside them. They soon arrived at the field where the fair was, and went swinging away to the east, following the road the silver-grey car had gone that afternoon.

They knew the way by heart, for they'd studied the map so well. As they passed the signposts they felt their excitement beginning to mount.

'Graysfield next,' said Dick at last. 'Soon be there, Timmy! You're not getting tired, are you?'

They came into Graysfield silently. The town

was asleep, and not a single light showed in any window. A policeman suddenly loomed up out of the shadows, but when he saw two boys cycling, he didn't stop them.

'Now – into Twining village, turn to the left – and look for the house on the hill!' said Dick.

They rode through the tiny, silent village of Twining, and took the lane to the left. It led up a steep, narrow lane. The boys had to get off and walk because the hill was too much for them.

'There's the house!' said Julian, suddenly whispering. 'Look – through those trees. It looks like a dark and lonely place!'

They came to some enormous iron gates, but when they tried to open them, they found them locked. A great wall ran completely around the grounds. They followed it a little way, leaving their bikes against a tree by the gate, but it was obvious that nobody could climb a wall like that!

'Oh no!' said Julian. 'What now?'

'What about the gates?' whispered Dick. Then he glanced around him nervously, hearing a twig crack. 'Did you hear that? There's nobody following us, is there?'

'No! Don't get the creeps, for goodness' sake!' said Julian. 'What was it you were saying?'

'I said "What about the gates?"' said Dick. 'I don't see why we can't climb over them, do you? Nobody would do that in the daytime, they'd be seen – but I can't see why we can't do it *now* – they didn't look too difficult – just ordinary wrought-iron ones.'

'Yes! Of course!' said Julian. 'That's a brainwave. Come on!'

## 20  *A thrilling time*

The two boys went back to the gates. Dick turned around and looked behind him two or three times.

'I hope nobody *is* shadowing us!' he said. 'I keep on feeling somebody's watching us all the time.'

'Oh, rubbish!' said Julian, impatiently. 'Look – here are the gates. Give me a leg-up and I'll be over in a second.'

Dick gave him a shove, and Julian climbed over the gates without much difficulty. They were bolted, not locked. He slid the great bolts carefully, and opened one gate a little for Dick and Timmy. 'Timmy can't be left behind!' he said. 'And he definitely couldn't climb this gate!'

They kept to the shadowed side of the drive as they walked up towards the house. The small moon came out from behind a cloud as they came near. It was an old house, with high chimneys –

an ugly house with narrow windows that seemed like watching eyes.

Dick glanced behind him suddenly and Julian saw him.

'Got the creeps again?' he said, impatiently. 'Dick, don't be silly. You know that if anyone was shadowing us, Timmy would hear them and go for them straight away.'

'Yes, I know,' said Dick. 'But I've just got that feeling tonight – the feeling that someone else is there!'

They came right up to the house.

'How shall we get in?' whispered Julian. 'The doors are all sure to be locked. We'll have to try the windows.'

They tiptoed silently around the big house. As Julian had said, the doors were all locked. The windows were all fastened too – well and truly fastened. Not one was open or could be opened.

'If this house belongs to Gringo he must be able to hide lots of things in absolute safety – bolted gates, high walls, locked doors, fastened windows!' said Dick. 'No burglar could possibly get in.'

'And neither can we,' said Julian, desperately. 'We've been all around the house three times now! There's no door, no window we can get in. No balcony to climb up to – no ivy to hang on to – nothing!'

'Let's go around once more,' said Dick. 'We *might* have missed something.'

So once more they went around – and discovered something strange when they got to the kitchen quarters. The moon came out, and showed them a round black hole in the ground! What on earth could it be?

They tiptoed to it just as the moon went in again. They shone their torches on it briefly.

'It's a coal hole!' said Dick, astonished. '*Why* didn't we see it before? Look, there's the lid just beside it. It's been left open. I suppose the moon was in last time we came by this part of the house. Why didn't we notice it before?'

Julian was uneasy. 'I definitely didn't see it before. It's strange. Could it be a trap, do you think?'

'I don't see how it could be,' said Dick. 'Come on – let's get down. At least it's a way in.' He shone his torch into the hole. 'Yes, look – there's a whole lot of coal down there – we can easily jump on to it. Tim, you go first and spy out the land.'

Timmy jumped down at once, the coal slithering away from beneath his four paws.

'He's down all right,' said Julian. 'I'll go next. Then you.'

Down they jumped, and the coal slithered away again, making what seemed to be a very loud noise in the silent night. Julian shone his torch around.

They were standing on a very large pile of coal in the middle of a big cellar. At the end was a door.

'Hope it's not locked,' said Dick, in a whisper. 'Now, Tim, keep to heel, for goodness' sake, and don't make a sound!'

They went to the door, treading on gritty bits of coal. Julian turned the dirty handle – and the door opened inwards!

'It's not locked!' said Julian, thankfully.

They crept through it, Timmy treading on their heels, and found themselves in another cellar, set with stone shelves on which were piled tins and boxes and crates.

'Enough food here to stand a siege!' whispered Dick. 'Where are the cellar steps? We've got to get out.'

'Over there,' said Julian.

Then he stopped and put out his torch. He had heard something.

'Did you hear that?' he whispered. 'It sounded like somebody treading on the coal in the coal cellar! I hope nobody *is* shadowing us or we'll soon be prisoners.'

They listened but heard nothing further. Up the stone steps they went and undid the door at the top. A big kitchen lay beyond, lit by the dim moon. A shadow rose suddenly in front of them and Timmy growled. Dick's heart almost stopped beating. What on earth was that, crawling silently over the floor and disappearing in the shadows? He clutched at Julian and made him jump.

'Don't do that, Dick! That was only the kitchen cat you saw,' whispered Julian. 'You made me jump. Wasn't it a good thing that Timmy didn't go for the cat? There would have been a terrible yowling!'

'Where do you think George will be?' asked Dick. 'Somewhere at the top of the house?'

'I've no idea. We'll just have to look into every room,' said Julian.

So they looked into every room on the ground

floor, but they were empty. They were huge rooms, ugly and over-furnished.

'Come on – up the stairs!' said Dick, and up they went.

They came to an enormous landing, hung with tapestry curtains at the windows. Timmy suddenly gave a small growl and in a flash both boys had hidden themselves in the folds of the long window-curtains. Timmy went with them, feeling surprised. Dick peered out after a minute.

'I think it was that cat again,' he whispered. 'Look, there it is, up on that chest. It's following us, wondering what on earth we're doing, I expect!'

'Bother it!' said Julian. '*I'm* getting the creeps now, being watched by a shadowy cat. I suppose it *is* real?'

'Timmy thinks so!' said Dick. 'Come on – there are lots of bedroom doors on this landing.'

They tiptoed into the ones whose doors were open, but no one was sleeping in the beds there. They came to a closed door and listened. Someone was snoring inside!

'That's not George,' said Dick. 'Anyway, she'd be locked in, and the key's in this door.'

They went to the next door, which was also shut. They listened and could hear someone breathing heavily.

'Not George,' said Dick, and they went on up to the next flight of stairs.

There were four more rooms there, two of them not even furnished. The doors of the other two were ajar, and it was obvious that people were sleeping in them, because once more there was loud breathing to be heard.

'There don't seem to be any more rooms,' said Dick, in dismay, as they flashed their torches carefully around the top landing. 'So where's George?'

'Look – there's a little wooden door there,' said Julian, in Dick's ear. 'A door leading into the cistern room, I expect.'

'She wouldn't be there,' said Dick. 'Wait – look, there's a strong bolt on the door! And cistern rooms don't have bolts on their doors, or even locks. This one hasn't got a lock, but it *has* a bolt.'

'Shh! Not so loud!' said Julian. 'Yes, that's funny. How can we get the door open without waking the people in those other two rooms?'

'We'll shut their doors very quietly, and we'll lock them!' said Dick, excited. 'I'll go and do it.'

He drew the doors gently to, and then locked first one and then the other, having taken the keys from the other side of the doors to do so. Except that one made a slight click as he locked it, there was no noise. Nobody stirred in the two rooms, and the boys breathed freely again.

They went to the little wooden door opposite. They pulled gently at the bolt, afraid that it might squeak. But it didn't. It was obviously quite new, and ran easily. The door opened outwards with a small creak. There was pitch-darkness inside, and the sound of trickling water from the cistern.

Dick flashed his torch on and off quickly. In that second he saw something that made his heart jump!

There was a small mattress on the floor of the little cistern room, and someone was lying on it, rolled so completely in blankets that even the head was covered! Julian had seen it too, and he put his arm on Dick's, afraid that it might not be George, afraid that it might be someone who'd give the alarm, perhaps another prisoner.

But Timmy knew who it was! Timmy ran

straight in with a small, loving whimper and flung himself on the sleeping figure!

Dick shut the cistern room door at once, afraid of the noise being heard. Timmy might bark with joy in a moment, or George might shout!

The figure gave a grunt and sat up. The blanket fell away from the head – and there was George's curly mop, and her startled face.

'Shh!' said Dick, raising his finger warningly. 'SHH!'

Timmy was licking George from head to foot, wild with delight, but extraordinarily quiet – clever Timmy knew that this was one of the times when joy must be silent!

'Oh!' said George, hugging Timmy anywhere she could. 'Oh, Timmy! I missed you so much! Oh Timmy!'

Dick stood by the closed door, listening to find out if anyone was stirring in the other rooms. He heard nothing at all. Julian went to George.

'Are you all right, George?' he asked. 'Have you been treated well?'

'Not very,' said George. 'But then I didn't behave very well! I did quite a lot of kicking and biting – so they locked me in here!'

'Poor George!' said Julian. 'Well, we'll hear everything when we've got out of here. So far, we've been really lucky. Can you come now?'

'Yes,' said George and got off the mattress.

She was dressed in an odd selection of clothes, and looked a bit strange. 'That awful old woman – Gringo's mum – found these for me when I was taken to the caravan,' she said. 'I've got a lot to tell you!'

'Shh!' said Dick, at the door. 'Not a sound, now! I'm going to open the door!'

He opened it slowly. All was quiet.

'Now we'll go down the stairs,' he said. 'Not a sound!'

They went down the first flight of stairs and on to the enormous landing. Then, just as Dick put his foot on to the next stair down, he trod on something soft that yowled, spat and scratched. It was that cat!

Dick fell halfway down the stairs, and Timmy couldn't stop himself from chasing the cat up the landing and up the top stairs to the cistern room. Nor could he stop himself from barking!

Shouts came from two of the nearby bedrooms and two men appeared in pyjamas. One switched on the landing light, and then both of them raced down the stairs after the three children. Dick picked himself up, but he had twisted his ankle and couldn't even walk!

'Run, George – I'll see to Dick!' yelled Julian. But George stopped too – and in a flash the two men were on to them, catching hold of Dick and Julian, and dragging them into a nearby room.

'Tim! TIM!' shouted George. 'Help, Timmy!'

But before Timmy could come pelting down the stairs from the attic George was shoved into the room too, and the door locked.

'Look out for the dog!' shouted one of the men. 'He's dangerous!'

Timmy certainly was! He came pounding towards the men, snarling, his eyes blazing, showing all his teeth.

The men darted into the room next to the one into which they'd locked the children, and banged the door. Timmy flung himself against it in rage, snarling and growling in a terrifying manner. If only he could get at those men! If only he could!

## 21 *Most unexpected!*

Soon there was real pandemonium in the old house! The sleepers in the rooms on the top landing awoke suddenly and found their doors locked, and began to bang on them and shout. The three children in the locked room on the ground floor shouted and banged too – and Timmy nearly went mad!

Only the men in the room next to the children were silent. They were terrified at Timmy's growling and snarling. They'd have liked to lock themselves in, but the key was on the other side of the door – and they certainly didn't dare to open it to get the key!

Soon the children quietened down. Dick sat on a chair, exhausted. 'That cat! That annoying, sly old cat! I stepped on it and it scratched me to the bone – as well as sending me flying down the stairs and making me twist my ankle!'

'We so *nearly* managed to escape!' groaned

Julian.

'I don't know *what* will happen now!' said George. 'Timmy's out there and can't get in to us, and we can't get out to him because the door's locked – and those men won't dare to set a foot outside *their* door while Tim's there!'

'And we've locked the people into their rooms upstairs!' said Julian. 'Well, nobody can get out of their rooms to help anyone else – so it looks as if we'll all be here till Doomsday!'

It did seem like a very poor lookout. The only people who weren't behind locked doors were the two men, whoever they were – and they dared not put a foot outside their room. Timmy roamed about, occasionally whimpering and scratching outside the children's door, but more often growling outside the next door, sometimes flinging his heavy body against it as if he'd break it down.

'I bet the men are shaking with fright,' said Dick. 'They won't even dare to try and get out of a window in case they meet Timmy outside somewhere!'

'Serves them right,' said George. 'Oh, I'm glad you came! Wasn't I an idiot to take Sally down to the kennel that night?'

'You were,' said Julian, 'I agree completely. The men were waiting for a chance to get Berta, of course, and they saw you, complete with Berta's dog, and thought you were the girl they wanted!'

'Yes. They flung something all over my head so that I couldn't make a sound,' said George. 'I fought like mad, and my dressing-gown cord must have slipped off – did you find it?'

'Yes,' said Dick. 'We found a few other things too – the comb – the hanky – the sweet – and of course the note!'

'They carried me quite a way to somewhere in the wood,' said George. 'Then they plonked me down in the back of the car. But they had to turn it and it was difficult – and I suddenly thought of throwing out all the things in my dressing-gown pocket just in case you came along and saw them.'

'What about that note – with the word Gringo on?' asked Julian. 'That was a huge help. We wouldn't be here tonight if it hadn't been for that.'

'Well, I heard one of the men call the other Gringo,' said George. 'And it was such an unusual name I thought I'd scribble it on a bit of paper and throw that out too – it was just on chance I did it.'

'A really good chance!' said Dick. 'Good thing you had a notebook and pencil with you!'

'I hadn't,' said George. 'But one of the men had left his coat in the back of the car and there was a notebook with a pencil in the pocket. I just used that!'

'Well done!' said Julian.

'They whizzed me off in the car to a fairground,' said George. 'I heard the merry-go-round music next day. There was a horrible old woman in the caravan; she didn't seem at all pleased to see me. I had to sleep in a chair that night, and I got so angry that I yelled and shouted and threw things about and smashed quite a lot of cups and saucers. I enjoyed that.'

The boys couldn't help laughing.

'I bet you did,' said Dick. 'They had to move the caravan away from the fair itself, because they were afraid people would hear you. In fact, I expect that's why Gringo decided to hide you here!'

'Yes. I suddenly felt a jolt, and found the

caravan we were in was being towed away!' said George. 'I was really surprised. I waved at the windows and shouted as we drove through the streets, but nobody seemed to notice anything wrong – in fact some people waved back to me! Then we swung in through some gates, and came here – and, as I told you, they put me up here because I was such a pain!'

'Did you tell them you weren't Berta?' asked Dick.

'No,' said George. 'Of course not. I knew there'd be no fear of Berta's dad giving those secrets away, because he'd be told by you that *I* had been kidnapped, not his precious Berta. So he'd hang on to them. And also I thought *Berta* would be safe, as long as I didn't tell the men they'd got the wrong person.'

'You're a good kid, George,' said Julian, and slapped her gently on the back. 'A – very – good – kid. I'm so proud of you. There's nobody like our George!'

'Don't be an idiot,' said George, but she was very pleased all the same.

'Well, there's no more to tell,' she said, 'except that the cistern room was really draughty, and I had to wrap my head up as well as my body when I lay down. And the cistern made awful noises – sort of *rude* noises, that made me want to say "I beg your pardon!" all the time! Of course I knew you'd rescue me, so I wasn't really worried!'

'And we *haven't* rescued you!' said Julian. 'All we've done is to get ourselves locked up as well as you!'

'Tell me how you found out I was here,' said George.

So the boys told her everything and she listened, thrilled.

'So Berta went to stay with Jo!' she said. 'I bet Jo didn't like that.'

'She didn't,' said Julian. 'But she's been quite a help. I only wish she were here now, and could do one of her ivy-climbing stunts, or something!'

'Timmy's very quiet all of a sudden!' said George, listening. 'What's happened?'

They listened. Timmy wasn't barking or whimpering. There was no sound from him at all. What was happening? George's heart sank – had those men managed to do something to him?

But suddenly they heard him again, whimpering – but whimpering gladly and excitedly. And then a familiar voice came to their ears.

'Dick! Julian! Where are you?'

'It's JO!' said Dick, astounded. He limped to the door. 'We're in here, Jo. Unlock the door!'

Jo unlocked it and looked in, grinning, Timmy rushed in like a whirlwind and flung himself on George, almost knocking her over. Dick limped out of the room immediately Jo rushed in, much to everyone's astonishment. Then he returned, looking pleased with himself.

'Let's go while the going's good,' he said.

'Yes – but, be careful, those men will be out, now that Timmy isn't there to guard them!' cried Julian, suddenly realising that the two angry men could easily escape while Timmy was in with them – and might lock the door on the lot of them, Timmy too!

'It's all right – there's no desperate hurry!' said Dick. 'I thought of that. I slipped out and locked their door on *them*, as soon as Jo rushed in to us. And they can stay there till the police arrive in the morning. Then they can collect the whole lot – the men upstairs too.'

'And I'm sure the police'll want to search the house and the cellars,' said Julian. 'There'll be plenty of stuff here that they'll be interested in! Well, let's go.'

They called a cheery goodbye to the two men.

'We're off!' shouted Dick. 'You'd better look out for the dog in case he gets you!'

They all went down the hall, Dick hobbling, for his ankle was still painful.

'We might as well leave in style,' said Julian, and unbolted and unlocked the front door. 'Also we might as well leave this door open for the police to come in by – I don't expect *they'll* want to come in through the coal hole! It was a good idea of yours to let the men think we were leaving Tim behind to guard them, Dick – they won't dare even to climb out of the windows in case he's waiting for them!'

'We've left a lot of lights on,' said George, looking back. 'Come on, Timmy, out into the dark, dark night!'

They went down the front steps and into the dark drive. Everyone felt safe with Timmy running ahead.

'Jo – exactly how did you get here?' said Dick, suddenly. 'We told you not to come.'

'I know,' said Jo. 'Well, I just took Anne's bike

and followed you, that's all. And I walked in through the front gates when you'd left them open, of course. That was easy.'

'I kept *thinking* there was someone behind me!' said Dick. 'And there was – it was *you*, you little horror! No wonder Timmy didn't bother to bark or growl.'

'Yes, it was me,' said Jo. 'And I followed you round and round the house, while you were trying to get in – and I thought you'd never see that coal hole – so I took the lid off and put it on the ground, hoping you'd see it then. And you did!'

'So *you* did that!' said Dick. 'I was astonished to see it. I knew we must have passed it before. So that was you too! You want a good telling off, you disobedient, cheeky little monkey!'

Jo laughed.

'I couldn't bear you to go off without me,' she said. 'It's a good thing I *did* come! I waited and waited inside that coal hole for you to come back with George – and when you didn't, I left the coal hole and got into the house. And Timmy heard me and came running down the stairs. He nearly knocked me over, he was so pleased!'

'Here are the gates at last,' said George. 'What

are we going to do about bikes? There isn't one for me.'

'Jo can ride behind on my bike and hold on to my shoulders,' said Julian. 'You take Anne's bike, George. We'll leave these gates open. The police ought to be pleased with us for saving them so much trouble!'

Off they went down the steep hill, Timmy running behind, his tail wagging happily. He had got George back again. All was well again in his doggy world!

## 22 'These kids sure
are wunnerful!'

What shrieks and shouts there were from Joanna and Anne when the four arrived at Kirrin Cottage at last, at half past three in the morning! Joanna was awake, but Anne had just gone to sleep. She was sleeping in Joanna's room for company and Sally was there too.

The stories had to be told again and again. First Dick, then Julian, then George, then Jo – they all talked without stopping, excited and happy. Sally ran from one to the other, and followed Timmy about – but sometimes her little stiff tail drooped when she remembered that Berta wasn't there.

'Look,' said Dick, suddenly drawing back the sitting-room curtains, 'it's daylight! The sun's up! And all the time I've been thinking it was still night!'

'No use going to bed, then,' said Jo, at once. She was so much enjoying this that she felt as if she never wanted it to stop!

'Well, I suppose it isn't,' said Joanna. 'I know what we'll do – we'll have a big breakfast now, a very big one to celebrate – and then we'll all go back to bed and sleep till lunch-time. We're tired out really – just look at our black-rimmed eyes and pale cheeks!'

'Joanna! We're all as sunburnt as can be, you're just making that up!' said George. 'Come on – let's get this celebration breakfast going! Bacon – eggs – tomatoes – fried bread. Oh, and mushrooms too – are there any mushrooms, Joanna? And lots and lots of hot coffee, and toast and marmalade. I'm ravenous.'

They discovered that they all were, and twenty minutes later they sat at the table tucking in as if they'd eaten nothing for a month.

'I can't eat anything more,' said Dick, 'and I don't know what's happened to my eyes – they keep closing!'

'So do mine,' said George, with an enormous yawn. 'Joanna – don't say we've got to do the washing up, will you?'

'Of course not!' said Joanna. 'Go on up to your beds now – don't even bother to undress.'

'I feel as if there's something I ought to do – but I can't remember it,' said Julian, sleepily, staggering upstairs. 'I – just – can't remember!'

He flopped onto his bed and was asleep as soon as his head fell on the pillow. In two minutes everyone but Joanna was asleep too. Joanna stopped to give Timmy a drink, and then he bounded up to George and curled up in the crook of her knees as usual.

Joanna went to lie down too, thinking she'd just have a rest, but not go to sleep. But in half a second she slept too.

The sun rose higher in the sky. The milkman came whistling up the path and left four bottles of milk on the step. The gulls in the bay circled and soared and called loudly. But nobody stirred in Kirrin Cottage.

A car came up to the front gate, and another one followed. Out of the first stepped Uncle Quentin, Aunt Fanny, Mr Elbur Wright – and Berta! Out of the second car stepped the sergeant and his constable.

Berta flew to the front door, but it was shut. She raced around to the garden door. That was locked too – and so was the kitchen door!

'Pops! We'll have to ring – all the doors are locked!' she called.

And then, from up above came a sound of excited barking, and Sally's head appeared at a bedroom window. When she saw it really was Berta down below, she raced down the stairs and scraped at the front door.

'What's happened? Where is everyone?' said Aunt Fanny in amazement. '*All* the doors locked? But it's ten o'clock in the morning. Where are the children?'

'I've got my key,' said Uncle Quentin, and he put it into the front door lock.

He opened the door and Sally leapt straight into Berta's arms, licking her face from forehead to chin!

Aunt Fanny went into the hall and called, 'Anyone at home?'

No answer. Timmy heard her call, but as George didn't stir, he didn't either. He wasn't going to leave George for a minute, not even to go downstairs!

Aunt Fanny walked into all the rooms on the ground floor. Nobody there! She stared at the remains of the meal spread all over the dining-room table, and even more at the dirty pans and dishes in the kitchen. What was Joanna thinking of? WHERE was everybody? She didn't expect George to be there, because she knew George had been kidnapped – but where on earth were all the others?

She went upstairs and her husband followed with Berta and her father. They were all feeling very astonished now. They went into Julian's room – he was there, then! And Dick too – lying floppily on their beds, absolutely sound asleep! Aunt Fanny couldn't understand it.

And then she went into the girls' room – and there was Anne fast asleep too – and could that be *George*? But surely George was kidnapped – then how – why – where . . .

Her mother suddenly put her arms around the sleeping George and kissed her and hugged her. She had worried so much about her – and now here she was, safe and sound after all!

George awoke at once. She sat up and gazed at her parents in astonishment.

'Oh – you're back! Oh, how lovely! When did you come?'

'Just now,' said her mother. 'But George – why

is everyone asleep – and how did you get here – we thought you were . . .'

'Oh, Mum – yes, of course you don't know half the story, do you?' said George. 'Oh, there's Berta here too – and your Pops, Berta! Hello, everyone.'

She was still so sleepy that she wasn't quite sure whether this was a dream or not. But then Anne woke up and squealed, and that woke Julian and Dick. They came into the very crowded bedroom, and soon there was such a noise that Joanna and Jo, in the room above, awoke too.

Down they came, looking very dishevelled, Joanna full of apologies. She rushed downstairs to put some coffee on and bumped into the two policemen in the hall. She screamed.

'Excuse me,' said the sergeant to Joanna. 'Isn't anyone ever coming down again? We're supposed to be guarding Berta.'

'Oh – you don't need to do that now!' said Joanna. 'Didn't Julian phone you last night – this morning, I mean – I thought he was going to.'

'What about?' said the sergeant.

'About the kidnappers. Everything's all right,' explained Joanna to the two astonished policemen.

'We've got George back – and oh, there's those kidnappers – you haven't been told they're all locked up and waiting for you, have you?'

'What *are* you talking about?' said the sergeant, bewildered. 'What do you *mean* – kidnappers locked up and waiting?'

'Julian!' called Joanna, 'the police are here – and you forgot to phone and tell them what happened last night. They'd better go to that house and get the men, hadn't they?'

'I *knew* there was something I'd forgotten,' said Julian, running down the stairs. 'I meant to phone, but I was so tired that I forgot.'

Everyone then came downstairs and went into the sitting room. Jo was shy with so many people there, and wouldn't sit anywhere near the two policemen.

'I've just been told, Mr Wright, that there's no need to guard your daughter now,' said the sergeant, rather stiffly. 'Seems as if the police are the last to hear about anything!'

'Well, the fact is that we found out that Gringo, who owns the fair called Gringo's Fair, was paid to kidnap Berta,' said Julian. 'He kidnapped George instead, by mistake. We found out where

Gringo had taken her and went to rescue her last night. You go on, Dick.'

'And we left Gringo and somebody else locked up in a room on the ground floor, and two other people locked up in a top-floor room – and we've left the front door open for you and the drive gates open too,' said Dick. 'So don't be too annoyed about it, Sergeant, because we really have tried to make things easy for you! We've rescued George, as you see – and now *you* can get the men.'

The sergeant looked as if he found it difficult to believe a single word! Uncle Quentin tapped him sharply on the shoulder.

'Well, hurry up, man – they'll escape before you can get them if you don't hurry.'

'What's the address?' said the sergeant, stolidly.

'I don't know the name of the house, or the lane it's in,' said Julian. 'But you go through the village of Twining, turn to the left, and it's the house up on the hill.'

'How did you find out all this?' said the sergeant.

'It's too long to tell you now!' said Dick. 'We'll

write it all down in a book, and send you a copy. We'll call it – er – we'll call it – what *shall* we call it, everyone? It's a strange adventure really – it ended with everyone fast asleep in bed!'

'I want some coffee,' announced Uncle Quentin. 'I think we've talked enough. Go and catch your kidnappers, officers.'

The policemen disappeared. Mr Elbur Wright beamed around happily, Berta on his knee.

'Well, this is a very happy ending!' he said. 'And I can take my little Berta back with me after all!'

'Oh no!' wailed Berta, much to her father's surprise.

'What do you mean?' he asked.

'Gee, Pops, be a honey and let me stay on here,' begged Berta. 'These kids sure are wunnerful.'

'WonDERful, wonDERful, wonDERful!' chanted the others.

'Of course let her stay on if she'd like to,' said Aunt Fanny. 'But as a girl this time, not a boy!'

George heaved a sigh of relief. That was all right then. She wouldn't mind Berta as a girl, even though she was a *silly* girl!

'Woof!' said Timmy suddenly, and made

everyone jump.

'He says he's pleased you're staying, Berta, because now Sally-dog will have to stay too,' said Dick. 'So *he'll* have someone to play with as well!'

'Shall we really send the sergeant a book about this adventure?' said Anne. 'Did you *really* mean it, Dick?'

'Definitely!' said Dick. 'Our fourteenth adventure – and may we have many more! What shall we call the book?'

'I know!' said George, at once. 'I know! Let's call it "FIVE HAVE PLENTY OF FUN".'

Well, they did – and they hope you like it!

## Celebrate 70 Years of

# The Famous Five

These special edition jackets of the first five books have been brought to you by Quentin Blake and friends in support of the House of Illustration.

CHRIS RIDDELL

Helen Oxenbury

COVER BY Quentin Blake

OLIVER JEFFERS

Emma Chichester Clark

Quentin Blake

# www.famousfivebooks.com

Check out the brand new Famous Five website.

Featuring games and downloads from avatars to
screen savers for mobile phones and wallpapers.
Enter our amazing monthly competitions and online
team challenges to win fab prizes, including
limited edition merchandise only available
on the website.

www.famousfivebooks.com
www.hodderchildrens.co.uk

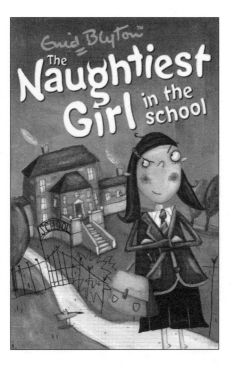

Elizabeth Allen is spoilt, mischievous and determined
to get home – whatever the cost – she really is the
Naughtiest Girl in the school! Exciting stories about
the girls and boys boarding at Whyteleafe School.

Hodder
Children's
Books